dual

Dispatches from Upstairs
Book Two

sara ruch

DISCLAIMER

This book is a work of,fiction. Gods and goddesses from many religions are mentioned. Some are based on historical and sacred texts, some are based on myths, and some are from the author's head. The author assures you she has nothing but reverence and appreciation for all religions, stories, traditions, cultures, and lifestyles throughout the history of both humans and gods on Earth and Upstairs. She thanks you for humoring her. This particular book mentions several real-life resorts and businesses. Any implications of nefarious employees or misconduct are absolutely and entirely fictitious!

For my real life MMC, Kevin

previously in dispatches from upstairs...

. . .

BEEN a while since you read book one? Here is a quick summary of Wake:

The story began with our hero: Chuli Davis, 28, long brown hair in two braids, hazel eyes. Editor of a tiny occult & new age publishing house, Burning Wind Press.

Chuli woke up disoriented and discovered someone had poisoned her with a magical love potion known as Veruni, and someone else had sedated and kidnapped her from a New Year's Eve party. Her mysterious captor, whom she nicknamed the Whisper, claimed he took her to prevent her from falling under the spell of someone else and helped her to safely navigate the situation. Afterward, her life felt newly dangerous and unfamiliar as she grappled with the question of who would poison her, and why.

Chuli was in the budding phase of a long-distance relationship with a charming author, Zach, but as their plans got delayed and her life altered, she became more and more attracted to the Whisper who saved her in the dark, especially after a hot and heavy encounter with him.

She reluctantly became equal parts fascinated and infuriated by her new co-worker, the bristling, beautiful, and mysterious Ram. She nicknamed him Scowling Man Bun thanks to the long dark hair he piled on top of his head and the nearly permanent sneer on his face.

She went on some weird dates. First, a double date with two Bollywood superstars: Ram's brother and sister-in-law, Sundar & Radha. Next, a baffling hike with Zach.

After a terrifying episode of a near kidnapping, frostbite, and a fire that destroyed her home, Chuli discovered an entire world that had been right in front of her the whole time. She learned that the gods of the myths are real. They originated from a place called the Upstairs, a patchwork of different communities not of the Earth. They enjoyed taking human avatars here on Earth, their soul occupying a human shell from birth onward. They forgot their past lives until around puberty, when somehow, the body could suddenly access their memories, known as their Knowledge.

All methods of killing gods were destroyed long ago, rendering their souls immortal. The nearest they could come to death was with a magical ceremony that permanently bound their souls to Earth, attached to unsuspecting humans for life cycle after life cycle, their Knowledge never to return. It was considered an act of suicide, and the gods who did this were called Lost.

They had their own supernatural law enforcement team called the High Order, who regulated the gods on Earth and kept their existence a secret. Chuli learned most of these things from her boss and close friend, Paul, also known as the Greek god Apollo, here on an Earth visit in a mortal shell.

Shortly afterward, she learned that a god of some kind resided inside her—she herself was a Lost. Other than a niggling sense of right or wrong which she nicknamed her inner fun-sucker, she could not communicate with whatever god was trapped inside her.

Around this same time, she learned many more things about herself: Her beloved departed father was actually her stepfather, her abusive brother was no blood relation at all, and her biological father had been killed in India, her birthplace, years ago.

Finally, she discovers that not only is Ram the mysterious Whisper and an undercover High Order agent, but he is also the Hindu god Balarama, and he had a heartbreaking past: His wife, Revati was a Lost, and he'd spent the past few centuries returning to earth again and again, determined to find her.

Ram struggled with his attraction to Chuli, who, at the time, did not realize that she was the vessel his wife silently resided in. He was both desperate to tell her the truth to see if anything from his wife remained, but also terrified he would lose her if she found out how much he'd been hiding from her. Now that he'd found Revati, Ram struggled with a fresh round of unresolved guilt and grief that remained from her original departure.

Finally, the poisoner revealed himself as a nemesis from the past: Revati's original intended, the one who caused her to be Lost in the first place. He was also Zach, the man Chuli was courting.

Although Chuli now knew who lived inside her, she could not access Revati, despite her attempts. Zach tricked her and drugged her with a second round of Veruni, then took her to the entrance of a mine she had shown him on their hike.

Under the spell of the Veruni, she was forced to perform a magical divorce ceremony on herself and Ram, who Zach had captured and tortured as well. Eventually, she found the will to kill their captor, freeing her from the effects of the drug.

With that settled, Chuli went back to Paul and his husband Stewie's house, where an intimidatingly large and gruff High Order agent explained the new rules: Her life as Chuli Davis was over, and she could not visit or live anywhere within 100 miles of her former home ever again. All humans needed to believe that Chuli Davis died in the fire, including her dear friend and former co-worker, Lucy. In exchange for her silence and as reparations for her losses, she was given access to a substantial bank account and a new identity with her true birth name: Naoma Bhatt.

After some discussion, Paul and Stewie, who had a second home in Brooklyn, New York, offered a new plan to help her out: They could move the Burning Wind Press storefront to New York, and rehire her as Naoma. She could stay with them and keep her job. Overwhelmed by their offer, she gratefully agreed, and then drove to Ram's house for closure.

After an emotional conversation with Ram, the two spent the night together. In the morning, Ram was gone, his wedding ring left behind on the nightstand. The High Order suspended him for giving Idun's Extract, a magical and highly regulated Upstairs healing potion, to Chuli to heal her frostbite, and for his failure to properly trace the Veruni to Zach.

Chuli, now known as Naoma, heard crying from somewhere and ultimately realized Revati was now awake inside her head, and very, very upset. Their night of passion had somehow unlocked the Lost goddess.

And now, let's begin Book #2, Dual!

one

$\bullet\ \bullet\ \bullet$

"YOU SURE YOU don't want to catch a breath with us?"

Even though Paul was walking right next to me, he still had to yell over the din of the crowd milling about the lobby. The rumble of voices blended with the music that seemed to bounce off every surface of the large brick and cinder block warehouse with its multi-paned glass windows.

"Nah, I'm good. I'll text you at the first sign of trouble. You guys go chill—I'll catch up with you later," I assured him, yelling back.

"With that outfit, trouble WILL find you, goddess! The good and sexy kind!" He called as they walked toward the blue light of the Ambient room, his arm around Stewie's waste.

"I'm not good! And you aren't either. You're tired and you know it. Let's go sit down!" Revati said, but I ignored her.

We were at Armagodden, a rave hosted by Dionysus himself in a massive warehouse complex in Gowanus, an industrial neighborhood in Brooklyn. Dionysus didn't throw very many parties these days, but when he did, they were legendary.

This was essentially my public debut as Naoma and I wanted to look nice, so Stewie and I had gone on a little shopping spree a few days ago. He found my dress at a vintage shop. He held it up and assured me it would fit perfectly, despite my objections. It was much tinier than the clothes I usually wore, but he was right. The stretchy, shimmery slip of a halter dress, with its open back and ultrashort skirt, offered little protection from the elements, but it was perfect for tonight. The dress molded itself onto my body like a second skin as I stood admiring myself in the fitting room mirror. I then practiced bending and stretching to make sure it didn't constrict—a fast getaway from any situation was important to me. As I did so, I asked him about his knack for finding perfectly sized clothing for me, like he'd done back when I had lost all my belongings in the fire. I wasn't expecting an answer—Stewie rarely talked. But he surprised me when he spoke in that crystalline voice of his.

"They put me in charge of dressing the virgins when the usual servant was accidentally dismembered. I quite enjoyed it. It was much more pleasant than scrubbing blood and vomit from the cells."

The clerk spared me having to reply when she bustled back in to check on us and gushed over the fit of the dress. I hadn't been brave enough to broach the topic again since.

Here at Armagodden, most of the crowd dressed in a similar state of exposure. It was much more practical for dancing all night in a warehouse without air conditioning. Even though we were a week into September already, the summer heat still hadn't fully backed down.

We'd already been here for a few hours, and dancing hard. A relaxation break would have been nice, but I didn't want Paul & Stewie to feel like they had to babysit me, so I blew them a kiss and walked in the opposite direction.

I pushed open the bathroom door, discreetly scanning my surroundings to make sure I wasn't being followed. I popped into one of several stainless steel stalls, did my business, washed my hands, and checked my reflection in the mirror. In the sharp glare of the fluorescent lights, I looked about as haggard as I felt. I splashed some cold water on my face, blotted it dry with a thin cheap brown paper towel, and wiped the mascara smears from below my eyes. I rarely wore makeup, but since this party was such a big deal in the world of the gods, I wanted to make a good impression, or at the very least, not look like a hot mess. I hoped I looked a lot better in the dim club lighting.

I ran my fingers through the curls in my newly shorn hair. It had only been a few weeks since I had dramatically hacked it off. Revati had been accusing me of not trying to look pretty enough. She said that I looked like a child with my standard hairstyle—two long braids. In an admittedly childlike fit of anger and spite fueled by a few too many gin & tonics, I grabbed a pair of scissors, picked up each braid, and hacked them at the base. My hair released into a choppy, mangled, chin-length mess. Revati was so stunned that she fell silent, and I picked up the braids I had always thought of as ties to my Lenape heritage, even though I knew it was an absurd stereotype, and tossed them in the trash. Now they were gone, too.

Those braids were the last link to my old life as Chuli, the little brown bird of Bear Mountain, daughter of a Lenape tribesman. As it turned out, he wasn't my father at all. My real father was from India. Both of them were dead, so it wasn't even possible to talk to either of them; to find out their reasons for what they did, to get to know my biological father and to learn about the man who named me Naoma Bhatt. I slumped onto the floor, a sharp and shooting pain in my chest hitting me hard. I sobbed away the grief as quietly as I could manage until it loosened its grip, then took a shower. Afterward, I searched "How to cut your own hair" on my phone, and found a video of a woman who had cut her hair from two braids, like me, and I followed her advice. I now looked slightly less psychopathic, with a cute layered bob. The extra weight I had cut off made my hair curl, which hid my poor haircutting skills.

The heat and sweat generated tonight made it even curlier than usual, so I scrunched it again, then reapplied my lipstick, a deep maroon the same shade as the dress.

"I don't like this dress. Why didn't we wear the other one? This leaves nothing to the imagination."

You know why. It was too long and constricting. What if something happens and I need to run?

"We could have gone to a better store, not just a vintage shop. What do you have against new clothes?"

I sighed. *Please, can you just be quiet for a little while?*

"Oh, am I disrupting your fun time, girl? So sorry." Revati was getting very good at biting sarcasm.

I'm sorry, I know, I feel bad for you; you know I do. But I need to pay attention. You know crowds make me nervous.

"Then why did we come here?"

We—I—need to socialize. I can't just only talk to you. I have to get back into society before I go mental. Besides, maybe...

But I didn't need to finish my internal conversation with Revati. She was secretly hoping just as much as I was that we might run into Ram, or at least Sundar and Radha. It had been 6 months since that day in the cave. 6 months since Ram left without a trace of where he was going or what he was going to do next.

I closed up my little bag and clipped it back around my waist. Revati remained silent for the time being, so I didn't know what she was thinking. She could read my thoughts and feel what I felt, but it didn't go both ways.

I was about to leave the bathroom when I noticed a woman staring at me from a few feet away. She was smiling a huge smile. I tried to smile back, though I doubt it was nearly as jubilant as hers. She approached and slowly reached out and touched my hair in wonderment.

"You are soooooooooo beautiful, sister," she cooed, touched my face, and pulled me into a tight hug.

For a moment, I panicked, and felt like I was back on the patio at the Chateau, where Zach held me tight against him while the Veruni spread through my body, robbing me of my free will. My free hand flew to my bag and the pouch on the side where I kept a paring knife hidden, just in case, and I gripped the handle on it before I stopped myself. Despite her haze, she noticed that I had tensed up. She backed away and placed her hands on my upper arms instead.

"I'm so sorry sister, you're hurting. I'm so sorry," and she hugged me again.

This time, I forced myself to relax, drop the knife, and hug her back.

"He's gone, girl. He can't get us anymore," Revati stated in a soothing tone.

It took everything in me not to cry, but I managed. I wondered if this woman was a god of empathy. After months of practice, I could finally make out people's auras; I could see just enough to tell the difference between a human and a god. With gods, the more they sparkled, the more power they seemed to have. Her aura sparkled a little, and she smelled good, like sweet earth and a warm cookie. People walked in and out on their merry way, most giving us smiles and approving glances. This appeared to be perfectly normal rave bathroom behavior. We parted and stood staring at each other again. She had long straight hair, gems glued to her face, some kind of hologram bodysuit with lots of holes, a lanyard with an ID around her neck, and loads of bracelets on each arm. She giggled and touched my face.

"What is wrong with her? Is she drunk?"

I sent a brief feeling of thanks to Revati for talking me through my panic attack and directing me back to the present moment.

High on something is my guess.

"Come with me," she said as she pulled me out of the bathroom.

We wove through the clusters of humans and gods milling about in the large lobby area. Many were standing in the line that led to the bar. I really wanted another drink, but the line was intimidatingly long. There were several rooms to choose from after this point, each with a different DJ and different style of EDM, or electronic dance music. Each style had a different name: drift phonk, deep, tropical, future rave, etc. I loved dancing, but I was more of an 80s new wave music kind of girl, so I had a hard time telling the various intricacies apart. I knew that the Ambient room, where Paul and Stewie had gone, was super mellow music. It was intended for relaxation and a break from the frantic dancing that took place in most of the other rooms, with black lights and an assortment of beanbag chairs and pillows. The spotlight room was the largest, and where the biggest headliners played. There was a metal industrial-style staircase with a large bouncer guarding the bottom.

"I want you to meet someone," my new friend said as we walked up to a man leaning against the brick wall, next to a fire extinguisher in a glass box.

Their outfits were similar, but his shirt had large sections of mesh. His hair was dark with bleached tips, and he had a huge smile for the woman. He looked young like her—my guess was they were both in their early 20s.

"Hey, Star baby, missed you," he said, coming in for a kiss.

They made out for an uncomfortably long time while I stood there, her hand still gripping mine.

"Get away from these weirdos!" Revati was disgusted, but I couldn't seem to look away.

It reminded me of the last kisses I had shared with anyone, but I quickly shut that thought down. Revati frustrated me, but I would not be intentionally cruel by making her revisit my moments of passion with her husband. Well, technically, he was her ex-husband thanks to me, a dagger, and two magic potions. Perhaps that was even crueler. They finally stopped kissing.

"Babe, this is my friend. She is *hurting*," she said to him, with a deep emphasis on the word hurting.

He stopped admiring her long enough to look at me.

"I'm sorry," he said with a surprising amount of sincerity.

"Thank you," I replied. I had no idea what the hell else to say.

"Could she join us? With, you know?" She said, petting his chest.

I didn't know what she was referring to, but declining seemed like a smart idea. I wasn't into swinging or threesomes or anything like that, but gods on Earth didn't have to worry about any of the usual concerns like pregnancy or disease that came along with regular human sex, so things like that were common in their world. Paul told me there was some kind of metaphysical High Order ju-ju that prevented gods from procreating here on Earth and provided immunity from external diseases. I thought of it as a metaphysical spay & neuter program. It was a relief to hear about, since I was ashamed to admit I hadn't once considered protection in my night of passion with Ram. It also explained why I never got colds or the flu growing up

—and here, I'd thought it was all those organic vegetables my mom fed me.

As much as I enjoyed sex, the thought of Revati being involved was enough to grind my libido to a halt. I wasn't sure how I was going to be able to be intimate with anyone again until our situation was resolved, which was pretty frustrating.

Before I had time to speak up and let the couple know I wasn't interested in that kind of experience, the guy said, "Babe, hurting isn't the right headspace for that."

Before Revati could ask, I inwardly replied.

I have no idea what they're talking about.

My new friend nodded once, like she made a decision, and turned to me. She took the lanyard off her neck and placed it around my own.

"This will get you into the VIP lounge upstairs. And this..." She pulled off one of her many bracelets, a black corded one with a pink quartz heart on it, and placed it on my wrist, "is for good luck. Heal soon, sister," she hugged me one last time. "See you at Introspection!"

She kissed me right on the lips, and the two of them strolled towards the Jungle room. I watched them leave, laughed a bit, and shrugged.

Kids these days.

"They're not kids, they're probably in their early 20s."

It's a figure of speech — never mind.

Now that I had the VIP lanyard, I decided to try it out. I suspected the VIP lounge had its own bar with a much shorter line. I approached the beefy bouncer. He was dressed in the quintessential tight black t-shirt and jeans, designed to emphasize his bodybuilder physique. His short hair was slicked back. He examined my lanyard, gave me a once over, and stepped aside, saying "enjoy, beautiful," or some such thing.

His breath smelled like mint. I smiled and gripped the

railing, glad my boots had low, chunky heels. I would have fallen right through the metal grate-like stairs if I'd worn stilettos. I followed the catwalk at the top across to a wooden door. I suspected that this was probably the original office from when they built the warehouse. It reminded me of every action movie I'd ever seen. I opened the door and went inside. There was a large wrap-around bar, dimly lit and well stocked, with only about 25-30 people milling about. Music was playing, but it was soft enough for normal conversations. Nothing untoward seemed to be happening. I found an open spot at the bar and the bartender came over. He also wore a tight black t-shirt, though he was less muscular than the bouncer. He had salt and pepper hair and a nice smile, and was very professional and polite as he took my order of gin & tonic.

While I waited, I glanced around for a more thorough observation of the other patrons, glad that none seemed to pay attention to me. I wondered what made someone a VIP at a rave.

"They're probably royalty," Revati explained.

"When I was young, they kept me separate from the commoners in a tent like this, with twenty women to wait on me. One would comb my hair, and..."

Tell me later? It's hard to pay attention to my surroundings when you're telling stories.

"You never want to hear what I am saying! Why are you so rude to me?"

I am not trying to be rude, I just—

"Here you go," the bartender smiled and handed me my drink.

"Thank you!" I unzipped my purse to get out some cash to pay. I should have had it out already, so I wasn't wasting his time while he waited, but I had forgotten while talking to Revati.

See? If I were paying attention—

"Don't blame me! You had already— "

"VIP is on the house," the bartender smiled and went to move on, probably eager to get away from the now flustered lady digging in her purse.

"At least take a tip!" But he had moved on, so I left a $10 bill on the bar and slid it toward the back so he could collect it later. I took a sip of my drink.

See how hard it is to talk to you in a crowd? It's really hard to focus.

"And that's all on me? No way, girl! Maybe if you didn't have so much to DRINK all the time, this would be easier!"

I sucked a huge portion of my drink through the straw, enjoying the burning sensation of the gin. I tried to visualize it taking my shame along with it as it went down. Yes, I really shouldn't be drinking as much as I had been lately. It was just that it helped to take the edge off my feelings a bit, which was helpful. At least I liked to think it was helpful. And it certainly wouldn't make me feel better if I thought too hard about how right Revati was at the moment. I needed every bit of liquid courage I could muster at the moment to get through tonight without having some kind of panic attack or making a fool of myself. It had been a long time since I tried to socialize with anyone besides Paul & Stewie or the rare friend they invited along. It was high time I started building a new life for myself.

I looked around again and locked eyes with a stranger. He had been in the corner shadows, and I had glazed right over him on my first glances. Now that I noticed him, I had no idea how that could have been the case. He was one of the hottest men I had ever seen. He was wearing a pair of tight, tattered jeans and open boots similar to my favorite old combat boots, the only clothing item I truly missed. He had no shirt on, but had a tattered, open sleeveless jacket, with many patches and spikes and decor. His hair was in a half-shaved, half-dread style, and his chiseled jaw had a hint of scruff. The sweat clinging to his dark brown skin enhanced his lanky, but well-defined physique. As I stared back at him, his eyes roamed and lingered over me before his mouth turned up in a lazy lopsided grin, as if he liked what he saw. I smiled back shyly, and he approached, stopping a few feet from me. He squatted down and picked something up off the floor.

"You dropped this," he said, slowly returning to standing.

He held out the bracelet my new friend had given me. She had said it was for good luck, and at the moment, I was feeling like it worked. I felt all kinds of feelings with him standing this close to where I sat. I forced myself to speak.

"Thanks, uh—thanks,"

He smiled a sexy-as-hell dimpled smile.

"Hold out your wrist," he said.

His voice was deep and rich, with a French accent.

"My wrist?" I asked, confused. I temporarily forgot the bracelet in the haze of his good looks.

He laughed, and his laugh was as hypnotizing as his voice. As he came even closer, his power seemed to send out little feelers. He was insanely observant. I should have been afraid of him. I suspected he was an Old God. He was exceptionally shimmery, but in a different way—like the glistening of moonlight. Whatever his power was, it had nothing to do with goodness and light.

"Naoma," I introduced myself as I held out my hand.

It felt like I was extending an invitation or an offer. Ever since what had happened with Zach, I had been weary of strangers, but I was quite interested in whatever dark promises that dimpled smile held. He slowly slid the bracelet back on me while looking into my eyes. It might have been the most erotic thing anyone had ever done to me. He then kept my hand and encased it in his. When he did, it was as if I could feel his power creep through me. It was almost painful, but also caressing. It spread up my arm and started seeping into my chest.

"Get him out!" Revati screamed, and it startled me enough that I pulled my hand back quickly, reeling slightly from the abrupt departure of whatever his power was.

"Sorry…" I mumbled.

He was still standing pretty close to me. He leaned forward, our faces close together, and purred near my ear, "I will call you Sugar, because you are a sweet thing," and he slowly pulled away from me, his face just barely skimming mine as he pulled away.

My body began leaning towards him of its own accord as I watched him lick his lips.

"Girl! Get away from him! He is bad news! No! Stay away! Get away! Run!" Revati screamed at me, but I stayed put and did my best to ignore her.

"Sugar?" he said in that French accent again.

"Mmmm, yes?" I crooned back.

"Don't let her treat you like that. Show her who's boss."

As my mouth hung open, he backed up, gave one last shake of his head like he liked what he saw and regretted having to leave, then turned and walked away and left the lounge through a back exit.

He knew. Holy shit Revati, he knew about you!

My mind was spinning. How did he know about her? Even Stewie hadn't picked up on it, and he was the most astute god I'd met.

"Go after him! Demand answers! Find out who he is!" Revati yelled at me, snapping me out of my stupor.

I thought you wanted me to get away from him?

I continued sipping my drink at a leisurely pace for a few more minutes, then carefully tread downstairs, gripping the railing as I went. Revati was pissed. I'd have to pay for it and apologize later, but if I stood close enough to the speakers, I could drown her out and have some quiet time for contemplation on this fresh new romatic development.

As I walked, I overheard a small group in front of me excitedly heading to the spotlight room.

"Introspection? He's the real reason behind the Maenads' frenzy, you know? Will said he taps into your soul until you lose your mind to dance. That sounds fucking gnarly. Let's go!"

Introspection was the same DJ my new friend was going to, and it sounded absolutely perfect. I hadn't been able to let go and truly lose myself to anything since moving here. I always felt tense and paranoid that something terrible was going to happen again. I even pulled my knife on Paul once, in the kitchen, when he snuck up behind me. I felt horrible, but he told me not to worry about it.

He'd pushed off the reopening of Burning Wind Press for months now. He claimed we needed to find the perfect location for it, but deep down, I suspected he thought I was still too messed up to pick up my old job and dive into work. I hated to admit it, but that was probably true. I promised myself that one day soon I would have a big long think and figure out what the hell I wanted to do with my life. I didn't want to take advantage of Paul and Stewie's graciousness & hospitality anymore. It was time to make some serious life changes, especially if Revati was part of me for the rest of this earthly life cycle, something we both cringed at.

I reached the spotlight room about the same time that my last drink kicked in, making my limbs feel lighter. It was dim, with some funky background music playing, and I floated through the thick crowd to get closer to the speakers. The air was alive with anticipation I hadn't felt in the other rooms. This was clearly the main event. The DJ booth was in the far corner, raised for a good view of the dance floor. It was currently empty. I looked around for potential threats and to see if I could find Paul & Stewie, my new friends, or that gorgeous man, but I didn't get far when the lights went black and the music shut off. A deep, robotic voice began speaking, though it was impossible to tell if it was in English-it was too distorted to tell. The crowd began cheering. The voice seemed to spin around the room, and tiny spotlights beamed above our heads. Some kind of ethereal synth sounds came on as well, building anticipation, until suddenly, the beat dropped, colorful lights exploded everywhere, and the entire crowd burst into a dancing, thriving mass. I knew right then this was going to be a night I would remember forever.

Introspection was incredible. I'd gone to quite a few dance clubs in my college days, but I'd never seen a DJ read a crowd like this. He unleashed an eclectic mix of genres and songs, all enhanced with beats and styles that made staying still impossible, with slow enough sections between so our hearts didn't burst from activity. We'd been dancing for what felt like minutes, but was probably more like an hour. I danced my way closer to the DJ booth, eager to get a closer look at the master behind the scenes. It was tough to see through the light show, but when the lights came down behind him, I caught his silhouette.

No freaking way.

Introspection was my mysterious, sexy man! The lights illuminated his face, and he looked up from his board. He caught my eye and smiled. I smiled right back. The song switched over. It was a remix of *Sugar, Sugar*. I laughed and danced to it, and my moves took on a different tone. Paul once told me whatever divinity lay within me came out best when I was dancing, so I tuned into it and projected all the lusty haze his smile produced in me into my dance moves. He may have thought I was sweet, but I wanted to show him that this body craved whatever delicacies that smile promised. A night of no-strings-attached, no-hearts-involved fun was what I was looking for.

The old me would never have dreamed of trying to hook up with a random dude, but the old me was dead— legally, anyway. I still didn't know who the new me was, but I was tired of expecting bad things to happen, and just drunk enough to stop worrying about what Revati wanted to do or not. Maybe, if I was determined enough, I could tune her out completely, or I could just blast loud music to ignore her while I did naughty, naughty things with that man. I would show her who was boss, just like he suggested.

Every time I looked up at him, he was staring at me with wicked promises behind those eyes. But somehow, he still kept the songs going, turning knobs and sliding switches without looking at what he was doing. I thought about the dude I'd overheard, the one that said he was the reason the Maenads went into a frenzy. It could very well be true.

I finally spotted my new friends nearby, and I made my way toward them. They were dancing close, still oblivious to my approach. Just before I reached them, they each took their pointer finger and stuck it in the mouth of the other. I've seen some freaky stuff before, but it registered as pretty weird. But they were sweet, and it was always nice to see friendly faces in a crowd, so I went to over to say hi anyway.

"Hi, friends!" I yelled over the music, but they still didn't seem to hear me.

I got even closer. They both dropped their hands and stood there, with not even a single sway to the beat, as if they could no longer hear the music. Both of them had faraway looks on their faces, and it wasn't a good kind of dream state. They both looked wide-eyed, shocked, and terrified. Something was very wrong with them. A feeling of great alarm went through me, and I called out to them. I shook them, but got no response. They fell onto their knees and then to the floor. It was hard to tell in the lights, but it seemed as if their eyes were rolling back in their heads and they seemed to foam at the mouth. I huddled over the couple, trying to think of any way to help them, doing my best to cradle their heads and keep them on their sides so they wouldn't swallow their tongues.

"Please, wake up," I cried, as I watched them take slow and raspy breaths.

I touched her face with the back of my hand in a gesture of love. Suddenly, her hand gripped mine fiercely, and her eyes whipped open. A terrifying flash of images crashed through me:

A man's face, handing her a paper packet with a stamp of a snake emblem. Two fingers, each with a small piece of paper with a dark stain. Pain, agony, disorientation, blackness.

As fast as the scenes arrived, they disappeared again. I reeled and came to. The music stopped and lights came on just as the bouncer from earlier and some kind of medic arrived. My friends had both stopped thrashing now but were unnaturally still, and the medics pushed me out of the way. I wished I knew their names, but it hadn't seemed important. The medic and the bouncer opened two small bottles and poured something down their throats. People were talking near me. One of them said what I'd suspected: The bottles contained Idun's Extract.

I'd seen what miracles Idun's had produced; It healed my severe frostbite within seconds. I took a deep breath, relieved that they would be ok in a moment. But the crew now seemed bewildered and a bit flustered.

The Idun's hadn't worked.

The man stopped breathing altogether, and the medic began chest compressions, but nothing seemed to happen. I couldn't stop staring at my beautiful friends. This couple, high or not, had been nice to me and truly concerned that I was hurting, and now they lay lifeless on the floor. They had both stopped breathing—it was fairly obvious they were dead.

My blood roared in my ears as I stood there, staring at their corpses. The current feeling of helplessness worked as a flint that struck inside me, flaring back to life those same awful feelings I'd been trying to escape since March. Had the man with the snake packet known what would happen if they took whatever was inside? They trusted him, and he let them die. I hated him fiercely.

I held onto that hate, a solid, icy feeling in this sea of flames, until the helplessness and despair were both smothered. I dug my fingernails into my palms to keep myself from screaming. I felt Paul wrap his arm around me, but I was now numb and stuck in place.

"We need to leave now, love," he said in a gentle tone.

"Wait," I said, though my voice didn't even sound like my own.

I pulled the lanyard back over my head and looked at it. It had *Star Dalim* printed on it. I pulled the bracelet off as well. I leaned down and placed both on her chest, then gave her one last kiss on the forehead, willing all my best wishes for a safe return Upstairs to her.

I took a deep breath and stood up again and looked around. Someone had forced the much thinner crowd backward. Most were listening to the bouncers trying to clear the room, but others stood around in groups.

There was a palpable space around one man in particular. The crowd seemed both excited by and afraid of him. They stared and whispered in hushed tones. It was the High Order agent from the mine, the war god who'd given me my new life. He wore a military tee-shirt, fatigues, and an assortment of weapons and other tactical gear strapped to his muscular body. He was standing about 10 feet away, staring at me.

He inspected me as if he thought I contained some kind of clues, starting at the top of my head, and going all the way down to the bottoms of my heels. It felt like a military inspection. I was waiting for him to reprimand me. "What's that scuff mark on your boot, soldier? Drop and give me 20!"

Paul had always called the High Order sanctimonious bastards, but after seeing two more lives lost because of yet another Upstairs drug, I thought *Inept Bastards* was a more accurate description. Before the agent could come over to talk to me, Paul took my arm and guided me & Stewie out the door.

two

. . .

LATE THE NEXT MORNING, I was doing my daily
long meandering walk around Brooklyn. It was a tradition
that started on the excuse that I was scouting for the perfect
location to re-open the Burning Wind storefront and to find
my own place to live instead of freeloading off of the two of
them. Paul & Stewie's brownstone was one of several in the
small, beautiful, and wealthy neighborhood of Cobble Hill.
It was a great place for privacy and safety, but it had
recently become so gentrified that homes and storefronts
were no longer affordable.

My usual route was a little further away, through
Carroll Gardens and into Red Hook. But Red Hook was
tricky—the sidewalks felt empty of the pedestrian traffic a
storefront would need despite the ferry to Manhattan, and I
could never really tell what was going on with most of the
buildings. Were they vacant? Were they for sale? A few
times I'd tried to venture into other nearby neighborhoods,
but this section of Brooklyn was not very public transit-
friendly, and I didn't like to spend time on any streets that
didn't feel safe.

My walks conveniently doubled as a great excuse to

get out of the house and learn how to deal with the voice in my head. It took a little while to adjust to hearing Revati's voice just as loud and clear as if she were next to me, and then replying silently, with my words formed as thoughts instead. In the early days of the move, I would frequently slip and speak out loud, especially when we got on a hot topic like why I still kept her a secret. That behavior would have sent tongues wagging back in my small town, but it was perfectly acceptable behavior here in the city. And if I kept my earbuds in, it just looked like I was on the phone.

Revati & I were both quiet and reflective this morning as I strolled through Red Hook toward the water. I wasn't sure what she was thinking about, but I couldn't seem to get the picture of the dead bodies out of my head. As I turned a corner, an unwanted flash of Zach's face as I stabbed him in the neck rushed forth, bringing with it the same feelings of heartbreak, guilt, and regret that had assaulted me before the Veruni had worn off at his death.

Anguish on top of a hangover was not a good feeling, and I reeled a little as I forced the mental and physical pain back down. I squeezed my eyes tightly as I braced my arm against a building to ground myself. I was almost recovered enough to walk again when a voice spoke far, far too close to me.

"Ms. Bhatt."

My eyes flew open in alarm, and I dove for my knife. Before I could grip the handle, a large hand stopped it.

"I hope you won't need to use that."

The agent from last night gently let go of my hand as I registered who he was. He patiently waited for me to collect myself. No easy feat—it took a good while for my heart to beat normally, especially now that I knew who he was. *The Executioner.*

I heard it whispered last night on our way out of the

rave, and I asked Paul about it. Once we were safely home, he was willing to explain.

"I don't claim to know the entire inner workings of the High Order. What I do know is that if you break the rules, you get sent to Those Who Judge. Whatever they say goes. There is no jury, no proper trial. If your crime is minor, they might issue a ruling against you. But if you violate that," Paul paused for effect, "they will send The Executioner after you. And then your Earth life is over."

"And that was him? Why was he there last night?" I had asked, trying to reconcile the deadly persona with the agent who had so neatly stitched my wound.

Paul had shrugged his shoulders. "I guess he does other stuff too, I'm not sure. I wasn't surprised that's who came with us to the cave when we reported you abducted, since at least one human life had already been lost, thanks to Zach. He must've already been on the trail. He showed up within minutes. But I WAS surprised when he was the one who followed up with you afterward."

"Why didn't you tell me who he was?"

"I didn't want to scare you further. I don't even know his name. Just his reputation. He never misses, and no one ever escapes him."

I brought myself back to the current moment, where The Executioner stood hovering over me, still waiting for me to speak. I took a shuddering breath, reminded myself I was just an innocent bystander, and started talking.

"I guess you want my statement? I just met them—"

"I know who they are. I know what happened," he said, his voice clipped and gruff.

I stood there, confused for a second.

"You don't need a statement?"

He shook his head.

"So, uh, why are you here, scaring the crap out of me then?"

I questioned, then reconsidered my words.

"I mean, I didn't actually crap. No poop came out. I poop just fine on my own. I just didn't hear you coming, you know?"

"Shut up, girl. That man could break you," Revati chimed in, oh-so-helpfully.

I'm trying! You know I blab when I get nervous!

"Walk with me."

I wasn't sure what else to do, so I started walking again as he kept pace beside me.

"Did they make it safely Upstairs?" I asked.

"It's likely."

"What do you mean, likely? And will they find each other? They were in love."

This was important to me. I was told that there was nothing left on Earth that could truly kill a god, and all their souls returned Upstairs once their life on Earth had ended, but it was still hard to believe without seeing. Dead gods looked, well, dead. Plus, the crowd last night had seemed particularly disturbed, so it would be comforting to know they made it back.

"Sometimes it takes a little while, especially after trauma."

Paul once explained to me that when gods took human avatars on Earth, their immortal past from Upstairs was somehow locked away, presumably so they didn't go mad while learning to navigate the human world as children. Around puberty, their past identity and all lives they've lived before, known as their "knowledge," would begin to come back.

Going on what the agent just said, I supposed the same thing must happen on the other side. I made a mental note to ask Paul about it later and thought about the trauma these particular gods had endured while I watched, their faces contorted in pain, their bodies thrashing on the ground.

"You know what killed them? It was in a paper packet with a snake on the outside. The man that sold it to them, that son-of-a-bitch—"

"Quiet."

Before I could get out another syllable, he barked out an intimidating command, stopping my sentence.

"You better shut up, girl," Revati stated.

What the... RUDE!

He stayed silent and kept walking, faster now, surging ahead of me. I struggled to keep up with his brisk pace. We walked around the corner. There was a limo parked along the curb, and we appeared to be walking toward it.

"What's happening? Are you trying to take me somewhere?"

I stopped walking, panic beginning to set in. I glanced around the street, looking for the fastest way to get away if I needed to. He stopped and turned around and seemed surprised that I was a few feet behind him now. Perhaps he read the panic on my face.

"Ms. Bhatt, I only want to sit and talk."

"I tried to talk, and you shushed me. Why do I have to be sitting? What do you want?"

"Stop! You're going to anger him further! Why do you do that? Apologize! He can kill us!"

The more Revati yelled at me, the less likely I was to listen to her, even if she was making sense, so I stood my ground, staring the agent down.

He looked pensive, like he wasn't sure where to start.

"Privacy. The limo is soundproof."

I hesitated. Could I trust him? I reviewed the facts. He was called *The Executioner*, for crying out loud. One didn't get a nickname like that from saving puppies and kittens. However, he had saved Ram back in the mine. He had also handed me an entirely new life, from a green card to a fully stocked bank account. Plus, he stitched my wound, which healed remarkably fast with just the merest hint of a scar.

"What's your name?"

"What?"

"Your real name. I'm pretty sure it's not Executioner. What is it?"

"Stop engaging him! Just be quiet already!"

Revati reprimanded me as the agent regarded me for a long moment.

"Webber."

"What's your first name?"

"Why?"

"Why do you want to be alone with me?"

Agent Webber regarded me for a long moment, as if he wasn't sure if I could be trusted with this information. He walked closer to me again, and I felt dwarfed in his presence. He was large and intimidating, but somehow, I felt if I just knew his first name, I could feel a little more at ease in his presence. His demeanor seemed to soften all the way down to his voice, which took on a surprisingly softer, smoother tone.

"Ms. Bhatt, please get in the limo so I can speak more freely. I don't want to risk being overheard."

This was probably as much as I was going to get. At least he said please. So against Revati's wishes, I nodded and finished the walk to the limo. The inside was quiet and comfortable. There was no one in the driver's seat, so I wasn't at risk of being driven away.

Agent Webber sat across from me. I stared at him while digging my nails into the inside of my palm, willing Revati to stay quiet. He noticed my white knuckles, then looked back up at my face, cleared his throat, and began.

"Are you good with secrets?"

I laughed a little at this. I had no idea what I thought he was going to tell me, but it wasn't that.

"I haven't told a soul about what happened to me, have I? Not even when my mom beg—" I quickly shut my mouth.

Stupid, stupid!

I was forbidden to talk to any humans from my past life or to go anywhere within 100 miles of my old town. I secretly kept in touch with my mother, Kunchen, anyway, because... well, she was my mom, and she lived over 100 miles from my old town. And here I was, ratting myself out for it.

"What did you just do!?" Revati gasped.

She knew he had implied there would be swift and deadly punishment for breaking my silence. He raised his eyebrow a smidge, and I felt the blood drain from my face.

"I'm not sure why you'd tell Kunchen about that former Burning Wind employee anyway," he shrugged, leaning back a little.

I let out a little breath as I digested what he just said, which was basically, *Yes, I know all about your mom. I know you still talk to her, but it's ok.* I blinked rapidly and looked out the window for a moment to catch my breath and keep from crying.

He cleared his throat.

"What I'm about to tell you is confidential, but I think you deserve to hear all the facts before you can decide what to do with them."

I hated to be in the dark and not know what was happening, which was exactly what had been happening to me so far this year, as I had been thrown for loop after unexpected loop. My mind still churned with all the secrets that had been revealed after the fact; I wasn't sure if my feelings about what had happened would ever truly be clear. It was refreshing to think I might actually have some proper information before it drastically affected my life for a change. I nodded again, a silent permission to proceed, curious about what it was I needed to decide.

"You're aware that certain substances from Upstairs are banned on Earth, yes?"

I glared at him. "I am well aware, sir. Have you made any further arrests or—whatever it is you do for justice—in my case? Zach got the Veruni from someone."

He had the decency to wince slightly. "No."

We sat in silence for a moment. When it was obvious I wasn't going to respond, he continued.

"The toxicology report on the dance floor victims was... quite disturbing. Besides the usual minor drugs and alcohol use common among our kind, it revealed a drug made from the blood of one of the more dangerous exiled creatures. "

"Exiled creatures?" I asked, my curiosity piqued.

"Yes. Most banned substances come from creatures too dangerous to be allowed to roam free here. They were all tagged, incarcerated, deported, or destroyed long ago."

I pondered this for a moment. I thought back to my dream of Ram slaying some kind of giant monster Upstairs. One of those things strolling around Earth? Terrifying. I quickly slammed that memory shut before it got to the sexy part.

"Hey! That is MY memory, you... peeping Tom!" Revati yelled at me.

I huffed under my breath. Webber continued.

"A drug that high in toxins could only be created if the blood was especially fresh."

I thought about what he said. If the blood was that fresh, it must be nearby.

"So you're saying you think this creature is here on Earth?"

"Yes. Echidna."

"The snake woman?! That's why the packet had snakes on it..."

According to Greek mythology, Echidna was half woman, half serpent. She had given birth to several mythical creatures and demons, including the Sphinx.

Agent Webber nodded and eyed me as if it impressed him I was following so quickly. I had a degree in mythology. If he knew the Buddhist name my mom went by, surely he knew about my educational background as well.

"Here in America, most banned substances are controlled by one large drug cartel. We've been keeping tabs on them for ages, but have an... unspoken agreement. As long as they stay on the fringes and keep the truly dangerous creatures off Earth, we're willing to let some things slide."

"Keep your friends close, but enemies closer and all that," I said.

He gave a brisk nod.

"What happened at Armagodden crossed a line. Echidna's blood is the human equivalent of fentanyl. Deadly. Dangerous. Stupid. This cannot stand."

I nodded in agreement, but then leaned forward, confused.

"Ok, so... why are you telling ME all of this?"

"What I'm about to tell you cannot be shared with anyone else, under any circumstances. Is that clear?"

He was back to his old intimidating ways while looking me straight in the face. I backed up a bit and nodded.

"We have someone deeply embedded on the inside."

"Oh, like a mole?"

That was about as far as my understanding of the world of espionage went. He nodded.

"His intel warned us that the cartel now possessed some kind of suspicious person, but until now, her identity was unclear."

"So they have Echidna, here on Earth?"

"We believe so, yes. But we can't act without proof. Visual confirmation isn't enough."

"You need DNA or something?"

He nodded tightly. "Exactly."

"I still don't understand what this has to do with me."

"Honestly, Ms. Bhatt, I'm not certain I understand either. Apparently, Echidna can only be approached by females, and the mole claims you're the only one he trusts. Some of our finest agents are female, but he insists it has to be you, despite your total lack of training and the perilousness of the situation."

"Thanks for the vote of confidence, Agent Webber."

I wanted to roll my eyes, even though unfortunately, he probably told the truth.

"Oh, you stupid girl. You thought stabbing people with sharp things was proper training for this?"

Revati chimed in, always eager to boost my confidence. I sat there for a moment, concentrating on my breath, so I didn't snap at either of them.

Deep inhale, deep exhale.

I was feeling a little calmer now, but I was still confused, like I was missing some important facts. It was nice to hear that there were respected female agents, though. Perhaps the High Order wasn't just this one alpha male after all. Agent Webber sat in patient silence. I suspected he was waiting for more of a response from me.

"So… this mole. Who is he?"

"That's confidential."

"You're asking me to go undercover and extract DNA from a dangerous serpent woman with an unknown agent who's chosen me somehow? That's — wow."

Agent Webber looked at me as he spoke.

"I can't tell you his name, but you already know him. And he has other requirements—safety protocols, if you will."

I cocked an eyebrow at him. "Safety protocols?"

"Yes."

He cleared his throat, seeming uncomfortable with what he was about to say. "He insists that this will only work if you marry him."

three

· · ·

I SAT BACK, shocked.

Marry him?

Whatever I had thought the safety protocols would be, they weren't… that. I thought of everyone I had ever met, trying to determine who could be the mole, and came up empty. I didn't know anybody from a drug cartel or anything close to it. Through my job and my friendship with Paul, I had met many gods over the years without realizing it, but I couldn't picture any of them as secret agents. And I had only ever met two High Order agents. One was sitting in front of me, and the other one was…

"Ram!" Revati yelled, nearly making me jump.

Agent Webber looked a bit concerned at whatever face I made when she yelled.

"It's Ram, it's Ram! It all makes sense!" She continued. "He's been undercover! That's why he hasn't been able to call. But now he is making things right again! He is marrying us again!"

I'd never heard Revati this elated before. It was disconcerting, and it was affecting my ability to think, as usual. I caught myself just before shushing Revati out loud, getting myself another strange look from Agent Webber.

"Why marriage?" I asked, talking a little too loud over the top of Revati's pleads that I agree.

"Marriage is one of the few things gods take seriously."

"They do?"

For some reason, this surprised me. I'm not sure why.

"Yes. It offers protection. As his wife, he believes you will be protected against any of the more nefarious ideas the cartel may have concerning you."

"Nefarious ideas?"

I got a very uneasy feeling in the pit of my stomach.

"Who cares! We're marrying Ram again! What will we wear?" Revati laughed and babbled on about Saris and colors and styles.

"These are not nice or just gods, Ms. Bhatt, but the protection of marriage is solid. Our agent believes an earth marriage is strong enough to prevent them from harming you, and solid enough to make your appearance justifiable."

"Earth marriage?"

"Yes. Earth marriage. It doesn't hold up in court Upstairs, but it is valid down here, and it is much more easily dissolved through human means, such as divorce or annulment. Upstairs marriages are a much bigger, more permanent affair, and almost never dissolved."

I felt a stab of pain over my scar and in my heart in general. Did Agent Webber know about Ram and me, and how I wound up with that injury? Did he know about Revati?

Revati got quiet. She was probably dwelling on the pain and shame of the divorce, or maybe she was fuming at my role in making it happen.

"After the evidence is collected, it would be your choice

whether you prefer to stay married, or you could divorce him. He will respect your decision."

"Why should I agree to any of this?"

"Money, for one thing. We pay our agents quite well."

I pondered this. Did I care enough about money to put myself on the line and jump into this crazy situation? He cleared his throat.

"Is justice a good enough reason? We don't have enough proof for a conviction, but I'm certain this is the same cartel the Veruni came from. You could help take them down."

Now, this was really something to think about. Did I want the people responsible for the lives destroyed by the Veruni and Echidna blood to pay? Hell YES I did. Did I want to marry an unknown agent?

"He's not unknown! I love him! He loves me!" Revati cried.

She could very well be wrong, though. What if it wasn't Ram? Would he really ask me to come into the fold and put me in danger? But what if it WAS Ram? Did I want to turn around and marry and then maybe divorce him yet again? Revati was obviously all for it, but my emotions were more mixed on the matter. It'd been 6 months since his disappearance, and he hadn't contacted me in any way, even to just ask a simple "How are you?" Could I just jump undercover with him like that, married?

"I need time to think."

I needed to meditate on this and have a serious talk with Revati, who was back to talking about wedding plans, without Agent Webber scrutinizing me. He nodded.

"The limo will be in front of your friends' place tomorrow at 10:00 am. If you agree, be out front, bag packed. If you're not there, we will assume your answer is no and we'll not ask again. Remember," He leaned forward again, in that menacing way. "This is confidential. Do not disclose ANYTHING that was discussed in this limo. There will be harsh consequences. Is that clear?"

I nodded in agreement, sufficiently alarmed as he doubled back down on his position of authority and menace. He opened the limo door, and I scrambled out and walked back to Paul and Stewie's apartment. They were sitting out on the patio, coffee cups in hand. I waved as I headed into my bedroom.

I got my earbuds. It was time to do some serious thinking, and Revati wouldn't let me be. I thought back to one of the books I edited in my days at Burning Wind about healing frequencies. That life seemed like it was about a million years ago, even though it hadn't even been a year. I opened my phone and found a playlist dedicated to the six solfeggio frequencies. I chose a song at 417hz, the tone dedicated to undoing situations and facilitating change. *Sounds about right.* I hit play and turned it up as loud as I could, as chimes and synth noises reverberated in my head. I was potentially damaging my hearing in my desperation to get some quiet time. Ironic, but true. I closed my eyes and tried to turn inward.

"Oh, this hippie crap again?"

It wasn't enough. Revati's voice still carried through my head.

Please, just be quiet. Let me think.

She must have tried, because I actually had 30 seconds of blessed peace before she started again.

"This isn't even music. It's so boring. You don't need to think. Ram is back. He will keep us safe through the mission, and then we will be together again."

Are you really that naïve? The last time Ram tried to keep us safe, he got himself tortured and nearly killed. And say the mission goes great and the bad guys get taken down. What then? I do what, exactly? Tell him 'oh Ram, by the way, Revati is awake now. She says you aren't combing your hair enough and your shirt is wrinkled.

It was a low blow, and I immediately regretted it.

"He will fix it!" She screamed.

"HOW?!"

I nearly yelled. Paul knocked on the door and popped his head in, looking concerned. I pointed at the earbuds and mouthed "Kunchen", pretending I was talking to my mother. He gave me a suspicious look and left, and I felt the guilt creeping up inside me. Now I was both keeping secrets AND lying. It made me feel absolutely awful, considering all the things that Paul had done for me. He and Stewie fed me, clothed me, housed me, and employed me. They had been on Chul—Naoma duty long enough. I had to give them their lives back while taking control of my own, and an option to do just that had just turned up. In the scheme of things, did it matter who the agent was? Honestly, my life kinda sucked right now, anyway. I was ready for a change, and I liked the idea of kicking some bad-guy asses.

I spent the rest of the night in my room, packing my few belongings into a single carry-on bag. When I came out to get a drink, Stewie was sitting on the sofa. I set my glass down and curled up next to him.

"I'm sorry I lied to him. I just…"

As always, Stewie just sat there, listening. Between his godly intuition and his bond with Paul, I was certain he understood what I was referring to.

"Just what, love?" Paul came into the room and sat down next to me.

"You two have helped me so much. It's not right to burden you any further."

Paul held my hand. "You're not a burden, love. You're our friend, and you just needed a helping hand to get back on your feet after something very bad happened to you. Don't ever think of yourself as a burden."

I used my free hand to wipe the tears from my eyes.

"So who was really on the phone, love? Was it that asshole Ram again?"

"No!"

At least I didn't have to lie about that. I wanted so badly to come clean, to tell them what was happening with Revati, who happened to be screaming at me to tell them at the moment. I wanted to tell them about what I was asked to do, High Order threats be damned. All the emotions were swirling and getting clogged in my throat, and then I was crying in earnest.

"I don't want to lie to you, so please...don't ask me. Not yet."

Paul sighed like a parent who was willing to overlook their child's poor behavior due to a greater love and concern for them.

"I'm leaving tomorrow." I raised my hand as if to block any questions. "I can't tell you where, but once everything is settled, I promise I will answer every single question you have."

I slid my hand over Paul's, trying to pump as much gratitude into him as I could visualize. "Everything you've done for me..it's incredible. I am the luckiest Lost lady in the world to have you, and you," I grabbed Stewie's hand with my other one, "in my life. But I need to go try to do this on my own for a bit."

———

In the morning, we walked over to Court Street to our favorite breakfast place. Finally, it was nearly 10, and it was time to leave before I lost my nerve. I gave them both tearful hugs goodbye and tried not to think too hard about what I was about to do. Revati was nattering on, wondering if Ram was going to be waiting in the limo, worried if he was, because it was bad luck to see your groom before a wedding. As usual, I mentally told her to shut up so that I could think.

As promised, the limo was waiting. My heart was pounding as the driver came around and opened the door for me. He was uniformed and looked to be in his 40s or 50s. He seemed like the silent, unobtrusive type. He took my single carry-on and placed it in the trunk while I climbed in. Inside was empty. I briefly entertained the idea of jumping back out, but I managed to stay put until the car started driving.

"So...where we headed?" I asked the driver.

"The airport, ma'am." He replied, as if he was surprised I would ask such a dumb question.

I supposed it was pretty dumb. Most people who hire a limo knew precisely where they wanted to go. I didn't know how much this particular driver knew about the High Order. I wasn't sure if he worked for them or a limo company, so I stayed quiet rather than explaining myself. Besides, what would I say to explain myself?

"Oh, it's silly, you see—the agent that arranged my marriage didn't tell me where I was headed for the ceremony," sounded insane.

I kept quiet and tried reading a paranormal romance book on my phone to pass the time, but Revati kept interrupting to tell me how much she hated my book choice, and that I should spend more time learning about my Indian heritage instead of reading fictional dribble. I gave up trying to read and pulled out the earbuds again.

"No, not that horrid noise again!"

I ignored her as I turned on some German industrial

music. It helped me tap into just the right amount of anger, angst, and apathy to keep me going. I was being a bitch to her, but I didn't know how to stop.

It took a little under an hour, but we finally arrived at the Teterboro Airport. We drove right onto the tarmac to a small, presumably private jet.

Holy shit. This is big time.

I was handed my bag, and I rolled it along behind me up to the ramp. The pilot and cabin attendant introduced themselves and escorted me onto the plane. I took in the 12 or so seats, side tables, wood-paneled walls, and overall ambiance. This was without a doubt so much better than my only other flying experience.

I was 14 when my mom and I went with one of her old boyfriends to meet his family in Florida. That involved huge airports, long lines, a crowded plane, and a cold reception by both those on the plane and the family off of it. They broke up shortly after. I think his name was Ron, but I couldn't quite remember.

Agent Webber was waiting for me inside, sitting in a heavily padded seat large enough that even he could stretch out his legs. I smiled at him. He cleared his throat and leaned down to pull some papers from a bag at his feet. I sat down in a seat across from him, a fold-down table of some kind between us, complete with cup holders.

"So..." I began. "Can I at least know where we're headed?"

"Las Vegas."

"Vegas? 'Like, what happens in Vegas stays in Vegas' Vegas?"

He raised an eyebrow a fraction. "Were you expecting someplace different?"

I thought about it and realized I had no idea where I thought I'd be heading.

"It makes sense, I guess. They are known for spontaneous weddings. I just thought it would be.."

I thought of all the romantic ideas Revati had in her head, and I knew this would be nothing like any of them.

"What is Vegas? I see strange things. Lights and..a Pyramid? Feathered wings? What is this place?" Revati asked while combing my thoughts.

It was wild when she described what my brain was doing from the inside while I daydreamed, and I wasn't quite used to it yet. I had never been there, so flashes of the Vegas I only knew from movies, tv, and stories must have painted a pretty weird image. I smiled as a thought occurred to me.

"Agent Webber, please tell me Elvis is involved."

He kept a straight face, but I thought I saw a bit of twinkle in his eye.

"If you want him to be."

"That would be an affirmative!"

I smiled a genuine smile, then quickly put all other thoughts of an Elvis wedding out of my head so I wouldn't ruin anything for Revati, who was repeatedly asking me where Vegas was and who Elvis was.

Agent Webber handed me a stack of papers, and we went over the details of the assignment. First was the astronomical sum I was to be paid—he wasn't kidding about the money! Next, we went over the rules of conduct of an undercover agent. It read like a standard insurance contract. There was a list of conditions where they would step in and assist if things should go poorly. It was a short list, mainly just different iterations of "here are code words about birds" and "so you got caught and they are attempting to torture/rape/kill you." It was chilling and disturbing. I tried not to dwell on it.

I was under a strict gag order. I could not talk about or tell anyone about my role besides my spouse and Agent

Webber. After the mission, I would be able to announce my marriage, but I was forbidden to disclose any further information about the case or the cartel under penalty of death.

The mole I was to marry—and yes, "I Married a Mole" sounded like an intriguing title for a romance novel— wasn't called a mole at all. Instead, they referred to him as "the informant." I was henceforth to be labeled as "the plant."

"I'm a *plant*? That sounds so... innocuous."

"Some of the deadliest poisons come from plants," Agent Webber said.

"Is he trying to comfort you by calling you deadly?" Revati asked.

Ha, I think so. Funny thing is, I think it worked?

This line of thinking got me wondering something.

"Do I get my own Idun's? Just in case?"

Even though it didn't seem to work on whatever the snake drug was, it wouldn't hurt to have something like that on hand, just in case.

"I'm sure since the ruling, you understand why that's not possible," Agent Webber said grimly.

I nodded, recalling our conversation in the kitchen at the Chateau after the incident in the mine. It was one of the reasons he was angry with Ram and thought he was a terrible agent: He had illegally given his Idun's to me, a human—er, Lost—err, non-High Order agent? I wasn't sure why it was such a no-no, but it had quickly cured my frostbite, something I admit I was quite grateful for. My fingers still had the slightest tinge of pink in some places. I couldn't imagine the pain and scarring I would have endured without it. I probably would have lost some fingers and toes.

The last time I saw Ram, he had been suspended for his actions. Since he had given up and left us, apparently there was some kind of ruling. I had no idea if he had gotten into further trouble. I briefly considered asking agent Webber, but it was none of my business. If Ram had wanted me to know anything more, he would have at least called, texted, or something.

"Could I at least have that magic cream? You know, that stuff you used on my cut? What was that? It healed so fast."

His eyes flared a tiny bit. "No."

I sighed. It was worth a shot.

We went over a few more details and an itinerary and agreed to meet up sometime after the wedding and before the mission began. Afterward, we sat in comfortable silence. Well, Webber sat in silence, and he appeared to be comfortable, but he showed very little emotion, so it was hard to say, really.

Personally, I had a whole other conversation going in my head. Revati and I hashed over contract details. She tried to pry more information about the wedding out of me, but I dodged her questions. Finally, she gave up, and I drifted off to the hum of the engine and air vents.

———

I am in the cave. Zach is there, and he is beautiful and laughing. He points to the slab.

"Look what you've done! Bravo, Big Bird!"

Ram is there on the slab, but he is dead, with a gaping wound in his neck, and blood dripping down. Instead of pooling on the floor, it drips over the charred remains of the waitress who died burning down my house.

Next to her lie the couple from Armagodden, their faces white and blank. Paul and Stewie are piled there as well, their eyes still open, still staring at me in death with a horrified look. All of them have deep stab wounds.

I look down at my hands and realize I'm holding the dagger. Zach laughs again.

"You've killed them all! Good girl. Now kill HER.

His voice is a command, and despite all my inner protests, I begin to raise the dagger, pointing it directly at my eye so I can stab myself in the brain.

"Ms. Bhatt."

Someone was gently shaking my shoulder. I opened my eyes, startled and disoriented, scared out of my mind. My heart pounded. Agent Webber was kneeling next to my seat, trying to wake me.

"You were yelling, Ms. Bhatt." Concern was etched on Webber's strong features.

I quickly looked away. I didn't want him to see me weak like this.

"Just a dream. I was at a gladiator match. You were winning. It was exciting."

I have no idea what possessed me to make up such an absurd dream instead of just admitting the truth. Though if Webber were in a gladiator match, I was pretty sure he would win. I looked at him and smiled and headed to the restroom.

"Was it the cave again?" Revati asked.

For some reason, she couldn't see my dreams. I considered it a blessing for her, since they were mostly just nightmares, anyway.

Yeah. I'll be ok. Just give me a minute.

I splashed cold water on my face and finished composing myself, then asked the cabin attendant for a gin and tonic before returning to my seat. I looked at Agent Webber. He looked back at me, but stayed silent and didn't push the issue. I forced myself to stay awake the rest of the ride while I nursed my drink.

———

Four hours after landing, I found myself in a fancy hotel room near the airport, made up tip-to-toe as a bride, thanks to the amazing and expedient wedding industry of Las Vegas. Who knew a bride could rent a dress and all the accessories and have them custom altered in an hour, and get their hair and make-up done while waiting? It was crazy to think about the months and years of planning some people put into weddings!

Revati was not entirely thrilled with my willingness to let the experts take the reign, but she was pleased that my fake lashes, eye shadow, blush, lipstick, and up-do featuring about a million bobby pins made me have some sort of semblance of a traditional bride.

"Ram will appreciate that you worked hard to look nice for him."

First of all...

I started, after finishing off the second tiny bottle I found in my hotel room's mini-bar. I was about to explain to Revati that a woman should not have to "work hard" to look pleasing to anyone but herself. I was then going to finish up with a second of all, where I, yet again, reminded her that we don't even know that it's Ram and cautioned her not to get her hopes up, but my conversation with myself was interrupted by a knock on the door.

I looked through the peephole. Agent Webber's large chest stared back at me. I let him in, and he gave me a once over, but it was difficult to tell anything he was thinking. I decided when this was over, I was going to have to expand my social circle beyond stoic, close-lipped gods, naggy goddesses, and my mom.

I'm such a lost loser.

Revati agreed and started boasting about how many friends she had at the palace where she lived. I cut her off.

"Show time?"

Agent Webber nodded and took my bag for me as he escorted me out the door and down to the limo that was waiting to take me to the chapel. It was located along The Strip, the stretch of casinos, hotels, fountains, and shops Las Vegas was famous for.

We got in and situated — not the easiest task in a wedding dress. He got me a bottle of water from a cooler. I inwardly cringed at having to waste so much plastic, but the desert air was no joke, so I took it and drank some; I didn't want to be dehydrated on my wedding day. As I was drinking, I checked out Agent Webber's outfit. It was his usual military get-up, but he managed to hide the usual array of weapons.

"You look very nice, Agent Webber. Army green is a good color for you." I figured compliments wouldn't hurt, even if they were slightly sarcastic.

He just stared at me and then took a sip of his own much sturdier-looking steel water bottle. Suddenly, a thought crashed into my head and my eyes went wide.

"Am I—Oh Gods, are you—am I," I tripped the words out, "marrying YOU?"

It made about as much sense as anything else in this whole arrangement. Agent Webber almost spit out his water. He managed to stop himself, but not before choking on it instead. After awkwardly watching him struggle while coughing and sputtering for a bit, I spoke.

"I'm going to assume that's a no,"

"You are not marrying me, Ms. Bhatt," He managed to grind out as he regained his composure.

I suspected The Executioner had even fewer friends than I did, but what did I really know about him? Nothing.

"Stop flirting with the man! It's your wedding day!" Revati chastised.

That was an honest question! THIS is flirting.

"I see you're pretty choked up about it. Maybe next mission," I said as I smiled and winked at him.

He just stared again. He may have even been blushing, but it was hard to tell since he was still not entirely over his coughing fit.

It was still daylight as we approached the strip from the outside. There was a tall cement wall and fences everywhere. Flashing signs, fancy hotels, and wild amusement park-like architecture jutted up from inside the cement enclosure. It felt almost as if the wall was some divide between fantasy and reality as we drove through to the other side.

I continued to stare out the tinted window. The bright sun felt out of place, reflecting off all the buildings, cement, fountains, and glass. I was reminded of the way a dive bar looked at closing time, when bartenders cut the music and turn the bright fluorescent house lights on at the end of the night to break up the mood and encourage everyone to go home, exposing the smeared eye makeup and the sticky floors for better observation. It was not a good look, and I tried to tamp my reservations down with good old-fashioned idle chit-chat.

"Do you like it here? In Vegas?"

Agent Webber looked at me as if deciding how much talking he was going to allow between us, or perhaps how honest he should be. After a pause, he finally answered.

"No."

"Stop ignoring me, girl. I'm trying to explain to you the Hindu parts of the ceremony, because I'm sure you'll be confused, but.."

Revati, I promise you, even if it is Ram, this will not be a Hindu ceremony.

"Why not! Why won't you tell—"

I closed my eyes and started to hum some Elvis to tune her out, but the only song I could think of was *Blue Christ-*

mas. I probably looked insane to Agent Webber, but I didn't bother to open my eyes to gauge his reaction.

Eventually, the limo pulled up in front of the chapel. Agent Webber helped me out, his huge hand once again dwarfing mine. He was still intimidating, but I was beginning to find him endearing under his brusque demeanor now that I'd unsettled him enough to make him choke on his water. Perhaps he had chinks in his armor after all.

"You're coming, right?" I said, suddenly feeling very nervous. I didn't know why, but somehow I felt like having him there would steady me a bit.

"To the wedding?" He looked surprised that I would ask. "You want me there?"

"I just thought... nevermind,"

I mumbled, embarrassed, and I turned toward the entrance, taking in the little white church with the cobblestone chimney. It felt a bit like a movie set. My heart rate increased, and my legs felt a little shaky.

"Ms. Bhatt," he called to stop me.

I turned back around to look at him. He took a step closer and spoke quietly, so the tourists clustering nearby taking selfies didn't hear him.

"You broke a powerful love spell and sunk a ceremonial dagger into someone's neck."

My eyes went wide as I realized what I must have looked like the first time he'd seen me in the cave.

Gods, I must've looked insane.

"THAT took courage. This," he gestured to the chapel," is just rings and a piece of paper and an Elvis impersonator."

I smiled at him, tears brimming, grateful for the completely unexpected encouragement. I could do this. I went inside, my head held high.

Once inside the chapel, I was escorted to a side room with a long white couch and a cooler full of flowers and told to wait for Elvis. Nerves began to kick in again, but I focused on Agent Webber's words. He was right. This was nothing but rings and a piece of paper and an Elvis impersonator. Right on cue, Elvis strode in, all smarmy smiles and a 70s outfit. I stood up, and he linked arms with me.

"Well, hiya, little lady! Let's go get your hunka-hunka burnin' love!"

We headed towards the chapel door, Revati getting more concerned by the minute.

"Who is this man? Is this a priest?"

I kept quiet and kept the smile pasted on my face, trying to focus on Revati's confusion rather than my nerves.

Prepare for some hip shaking!

"Hip shaking? Why? What is this? A… sex church?"

Hah, not quite.

We paused in the back, just around the corner, waiting for the music to change to the song I would walk down the aisle to. I couldn't see down the aisle to the front yet, but there was exactly one person in the back — Agent Webber.

He was just outside of the doorway across from me that led to some kind of courtyard, and was just barely visible. My guess was he was trying to avoid the photographer, which made sense. It's probably not cool to have photographs out there of a High Order officer at the wedding of folks going deep undercover, and he would have been incredibly conspicuous in the small chapel with its low benches. He probably shouldn't be here at all, and it looked like he knew it. I had a feeling he only was because I had asked him. I smiled and bowed my head as I tried to project my gratitude, and he gave a slight nod.

Finally, the current song ended, and we stepped forward and turned right when we got to the aisle. We began the slow march, with Elvis singing *Love me Tender*. We stopped halfway down for a photo.

I looked at the groom, and my heart began pounding wildly. I had to focus on taking deep breaths.

"Stop! Stop! No! NOOOO!"

Revati was screaming in my head as I locked eyes with my intended. He smiled as if he knew precisely how alarmed she was. He definitely knew. Because he was the only other soul that knew about my issues with Revati.

four

. . .

THE MAN I only knew as Introspection continued to stare at me as we got to the altar, stopping for a few more photos along the way. I had wanted to get to know him better, but this? Was this really happening? *It's not too late. I can stop this,* I thought.

"Yes, please! Please, Naoma! We were tricked! This is not Ram! They lied!"

But something in his gaze kept me heading toward him. It appeared part plead, part dare to see this through.

Rings, a piece of paper, and an Elvis impersonator. Fuck it. We're doing this.

The next few minutes were a blur. Elvis began his soliloquy on the power of love with a few popular lyrics thrown in for good measure, and then he sang one more song. I hardly understood what he was saying.

I couldn't stop staring at the man in front of me. He was dressed immaculately in a tight blue suit that seemed African in design. He was absolutely gorgeous. His hands were placed on mine while I awkwardly held onto my silk bouquet. This time, his power felt slightly different. It was lighter somehow, almost gentler, softer, even soothing, without that hint of wickedness. *Weird.*

"So now it's time," Elvis said, bringing me back to the moment, "for your vows. Pierre, you'll go first. Please reply after each question with 'I do'."

His name is Pierre! Huh. I just learned my future husband's first name from an Elvis impersonator during our wedding vows.

That thought was so absurd that a slightly demented-sounding laugh escaped my lips. Elvis looked concerned and paused. I sent him an apologetic smile, and he went back to addressing Pierre.

"Pierre, do you take Naoma to be your lawfully wedded wife?"

"I do."

"Do you promise to love, honor, and cherish her, in sickness and in health?"

"I do."

"And do you promise to protect her for as long as you both shall live?"

"I do."

Each time he said the words, he looked straight into my eyes, and damn if he didn't look like he meant it. Now it was my turn.

"Naoma, do you take Pierre to be your lawfully wedded husband?"

"I do."

"Do you promise to love, honor, and cherish him, in sickness and in health?"

"I do."

"And do you promise to hold only onto him, for as long as you both shall live?"

At these words, Revati began sobbing. My heart broke a bit for her. She truly, deeply loved Ram with all her heart. But there was no turning back now. Pierre gave my hands a gentle squeeze, and I swallowed the lump forming in my throat.

"I do."

Elvis quite literally jumped, with another hip shake for good measure, into another speech about our love. We then proceeded through the ring ceremony. Thankfully, Pierre had rings for both of us. His ring was black metal of some kind, and it was actually two bands clipped together. Mine was a set as well: an engagement ring with what I assumed was a series of diamonds and another band that had some kind of dark sparkling gems inset in the band. I was going to have to inspect both later.

"And now, from my movie *Blue Hawaii*…"

Elvis launched into a karaoke version of *Can't Help Falling in Love*, music being pumped in from the speakers. It was time for our first dance. Introspection—Pierre, wrapped his arms around my waist, and I wrapped mine around his shoulders. Together, we slow-danced, as the resident photographer/videographer slowly circled us for the best angle. He leaned in, his lips nearly brushing my ear as he whispered.

"Thank you for saying yes. Are you ok?"

Internally, I seemed to be alternating wildly between thinking this was a grand adventure and thinking this was a terrible mistake, but damn if he wasn't being an absolute sweetheart to me, which pushed me to nod.

"Is she ok?"

I shook my head no. Revati was definitely not ok with any of this. He leaned back a bit so he could look at my face. It was as if he could read right into me.

Then he leaned in again and said, "I can help both of you, I promise. I know how to fix this. But you have to trust me. Can you do that?"

I studied his face. I was so tired of having my guard up

after this whole year, and I desperately wanted someone who I could trust.

"I don't trust him!" Revati cried.

We're just going to have to try. We can't keep on like this.

She didn't have a response to that. I nodded.

"Take the wheel, Pierre."

Whatever he saw in my face when I said that delighted him, and he smiled the most adorable dimpled smile yet.

"And now, ladies and gentlemen, it's time for some more vows, Elvis-style!"

We repeated after Elvis some more, with awful vows that included blue suede shoes and teddy bears and jailhouses.

"You may now kiss the bride!" Elvis announced.

Pierre smiled again, and then his mouth was on mine. His lips were soft and smooth. I opened to him, and our kiss escalated into something more carnal as he pulled me a little closer into him. Now that we were this close, I could feel his power trying to creep up into me, but he seemed to be trying to hold it back. He was a very, *very* good kisser.

Elvis droned on about love yet again, as if he hadn't already said enough. He cleared his throat, and we stopped kissing to look at each other again. His kiss had released enough giddiness inside me that I was no longer panicked, and a wicked smile bloomed on my lips.

"May I now present to you Mr. And Mrs..." Elvis took the mic and held it out towards us.

Pierre leaned into the mic and said, "Sugar," and smiled at me again.

"Mr. & Mrs. Sugar!" Elvis repeated as he laughed.

The grand finale of the wedding was dancing to *Viva Las Vegas*. He grabbed me around the waist, and we somehow pulled off some seriously awesome dance moves.

Oh yes, this is going to be fun!

sara ruch

We walked out of the chapel hand in hand. I blew a kiss to Agent Webber and mouthed "thank you". He gave me a little smirk and then a menacing glance to Introspection, and then we were out the door and in the limo.

Apparently, the limo driver knew more about our destination than I did, since I had no idea where we were going. Revati began screaming at me for being so reckless.

You were all on board with this too. I tried to tell you it might not be Ram.

"It is exhausting, no?" My new husband asked.

I didn't really know how to answer that, so I changed the subject.

"What do you want me to call you? Pierre? Introspection? Something else?"

He pondered this for a moment. "I am simply known as Introspection, or Intro. It did not feel appropriate for our wedding vows, so I permitted Elvis to use a given name. If I had known Agent Webber would insist on attending the ceremony, I wouldn't have allowed it."

He looked annoyed that Agent Webber was there.

"He didn't know your first name? But he's like, your co-worker or something, isn't he?" I was confused.

"I don't work for the High Order." He laughed a little. "I hate most of those pricks. I only help them when the balance is threatened. And I only talk to Agent Webber."

I began to panic a bit.

If both Introspection and Paul hated the High Order, what the hell had I just done with those contracts earlier today? Did I just hand my soul over to a bunch of bastards?

As if he could see the wheels turning, Introspection leaned in close to me and affectionately ran the back of his hand across my cheek.

"Sugar, there's a reason I went to them for this. They will offer you the best protection on Earth. I don't like

56

them, but you are safe with them if something happens to me."

I swallowed hard. "And I can really trust you?"

I felt him nod his head. "You really can."

"How do I know?"

The limo had stopped, and the door opened just as I spoke. "Because we are going to trust you back. Come see."

We?

I wondered, but now was not the time to ask, since he was helping me get out of the limo before grabbing my bag. We were in front of a fancy-looking hotel. Once the limo driver pulled away, I followed Introspection up the street a bit, where we walked into a parking garage, my carry-on bag rolling along the cement, the sound bouncing off the underground walls.

We walked up a ramp and around a corner, and then I saw our destination. "JUST MARRIED" was painted on the back window of an immaculate 70s muscle car. My heart sped up just to gaze at it.

"Is that…"

"Our ride. You like it?"

"Do I...like it?"

I approached it with reverence, and slowly and gently traced the chrome wave emblem on the side as I spoke.

"This is a Pierre Cardin Javelin," I gaped at him. "'72 or '73?"

He laughed. "'73."

"So it's AMX, not SST. 360 or 401?"

"401."

I admired what appeared to be the original paint job. "Fresh plum?"

He laughed again. "If you say so. I take it you know your cars. That's all I know about it. I liked its look, and it has my given name on it. And now it's yours, too."

He held out the keys and gently placed them in my shaky hand.

"This is my dream car," I stated.

My voice sounded strange even to me. I couldn't believe the odds. As a child growing up in my dad's garage, I would page through car magazines. There was a write-up about the Javelin, with the interior designed by the famous French designer Pierre Cardin. I had stared longingly at the pictures of the wild, bold colored stripes that ran along the seats and even onto the headliner.

My dad thought it was the ugliest car he'd ever seen, but I promised him one day, I'd have my very own. He said when the day came that it happened, he'd buy me a pair of fuzzy dice to hang from the mirror. I'd looked for one a few times ever since I'd gotten my license, but there had been less than 5,000 ever produced, and the Northeast United States is notoriously harsh on cars, turning them into rust buckets, so I never did find one in my price range that I could restore.

And now here I stood, in the dry desert air of Nevada, in a shady parking garage, unlocking the passenger side door, running my hands along the seat and the interior, admiring the shiny hologram-looking dashboard and the original 8-track player. No fuzzy dice were hanging, but I still felt the presence of my dad, anyway. He'd be so tickled for me.

Introspection took the keys back to unlock the trunk, and he placed my bag inside. Then he tossed the keys back to me with a smile.

"You drive."

I jumped out of the passenger seat, nearly tripping over my wedding dress in the process, but it barely slowed me down. I gently placed my high heels in the back seat and climbed in, hitching my skirt up as high as I could get it, exposing a few inches of my thighs. I did not want to get tangled in the thing and crash. I adjusted my seat, turned the key, and the engine roared right up.

"Oooh," I groaned in pleasure.

So far, the car was even better than I imagined. I adjusted my seatbelt and caught Introspection staring at me.

"This really is your dream car, Sugar?"

I smiled and nodded. "It really is. Since childhood."

He shook his head slightly, then leaned towards me. He spoke just loud enough that I could hear him over the engine.

"I would like to hear you groan like that for me, perhaps," he licked his lips, and I felt a hot flush creep throughout me.

I backed out of the parking spot and carefully cruised to the exit.

After a 20 minute drive that left me exhilarated, Revati screaming and terrified, and Introspection slightly alarmed at my increasing willingness to test the speed and dexterity of the car, we pulled into the driveway of a small stucco house in the next-door city of Henderson, Nevada.

It had a built-in garage and a red Spanish-tiled roof. Two big pine trees flanked each side, creating some much-needed dappled shade over the patchy lawn. I'm not sure why, but the pine trees surprised me. I guess I had thought Vegas was all lights and cement and palm trees. I put my shoes back on so I wouldn't burn my feet and we walked up the hot sidewalk to the front door, where he picked me up and carried me over the threshold.

"Welcome home, Sugar." he muttered while kissing my cheek.

I couldn't help but smile as I pulled in closer to him, feeling his lithe body against mine. I heard footsteps, and I turned away from him to look at whoever was approaching.

I've officially lost my mind.

An exact copy of the man I just married approached, giving me that same dimpled smile.

five

. . .

"I DON'T..." I mumbled.

Revati gasped. I felt all the blood drain from my face and my skin break out in a cold sweat.

"Elle va vomir! Vite, la salle de bain!" the second Introspection yelled.

I was placed in the doorway of a small powder room, where I slammed the door and then hovered over the toilet, heaving. I hadn't eaten since breakfast this morning. I did some quick mental math and determined that given the 3 hour time change, that was at least 12 hours ago, so fortunately, the only thing that came up was water. When the initial wave of nausea passed, I sat on the floor and leaned against the wall, feeling the bumpy texture of the beige wallpaper. The room had a sink, a toilet, a mirror, and little else. It was spotless, as if no one used it. I closed my eyes and remembered the last time I had been sick.

Memories assaulted me—of learning my house burned down, learning that a woman died because of me.

Ram, whom I had just learned was the Whisper, had come in and comforted me and shown me his greenhouse. I could almost smell him as I sunk into the memory and recalled what it felt like to be comforted by him.

Revati started crying again. "He should be here, helping us. Not… them. Why, girl? Why did he leave us?"

I'm sorry you got your hopes up, I really am. I tried to warn you.

Our self-pitying reverie was interrupted by a gentle knock at the door. Startled, I looked around and got my bearings again.

"Sugar, are you ok?" a gentle voice whispered at the door.

There were two of them, right? Did I hallucinate that?

"No, there were two of them, girl," Revati confirmed.

Ok, not hallucinating. There are two of them.

Although confirmation from the voice in my head was probably not the most reliable.

"We will explain everything to you as soon as you are well."

"I'm… just give me a second," I said, as I hauled myself off the floor.

I looked in the mirror at the sink and a hot mess looked back at me—fake eyelashes, running mascara, the works. I used the hand soap and washed the makeup off my face, throwing the fake lashes in the trash. I rinsed my mouth out as best I could, and attempted to pull the bobby pins out of my hair, but it had so much hairspray, it would have looked absurd if I took them out, so I left them be. I felt better, but I still wasn't fully going to feel like myself until I got some food and a shower.

Or maybe I will never feel like myself again.

That kind of introspection wasn't the kind that could give me any answers right now. I took several steadying breaths while Revati tried to rush me, and I went out into the hallway.

Introspection—which one, I wasn't sure—was waiting

outside the bathroom for me with a cold can of ginger ale. He opened the tab, and it made a satisfying fizz.

"For your stomach," he said.

I took the can and followed him down the hall. We passed by a cute modern galley kitchen with a breakfast nook into an adjoining living room, where the other Introspection was waiting. This one was lounging on the left side of the sofa as if it were a throne, wearing a pair of ripped jeans and a dark t-shirt. I guessed this wasn't the one I had married. The one still in the suit gestured for me to sit in the middle, and he sat down to my left.

I cleared my throat and took a sip of ginger ale. It felt really good going down my throat. So far, Revati was the only one asking questions, and I was doing my best to tell her to shut up internally so I could enjoy the soda for a second.

"Does she ever stop talking?" The Introspection on my right finally asked.

I shook my head.

"Never."

I placed the can on the glass coffee table.

"So...you are twins?"

I guessed that was as good as any place to start.

"This time around, yes. Not always."

The Introspection on my left said in a quieter voice. I tuned into him and tried to feel his power. As if he knew what I was trying to do, he offered me his hand. I noticed the set of two wedding rings were divided, and each of them wore one of the two bands from the ceremony.

When I made contact, placing my hand in his, his power was light and warm, the same power from the wedding. It reminded me of sunshine and cookies and all good things. It was the exact opposite of what I remembered from the club.

I dragged my hand from his grasp and turned to my

right and repeated the procedure. This time it was that same dark and sinful power that had disturbed Revati so much. I bit my lip a little. I liked this dark power. Reluctantly, I pulled my hand from his.

"So which of you is Introspection, and which is Pierre?"

They spoke at the exact same time. One of them said, "we are both" while the other said, "we are neither."

"Ok, well, that clears it up then," I said.

The one on my left explained further.

"Upstairs, we are connected in a way that is hard to explain. We are different, but the same. We do not separate. We are two parts that make a whole."

"Like the sun and the moon, or a yin yang?" I asked.

"Yes and no. Like I said, difficult to explain."

I thought about all the mythical gods and goddesses I'd learned about in many of the religions I'd studied. Dualism was a theme throughout many of them: the balance in the cosmos between the good and the bad—benevolence vs malevolence.

"I understand dual natures, or at least the idea of them. Do you have separate names?"

"Upstairs, we have many names, but none of them are spoken anymore. In our current human forms, we have one passport, one identity. Legally, we are Pierre Mebiame. We go by Introspection. We don't need separate identities," the one on the left explained. His voice was soothing and peaceful.

"No one else has ever seen us together in this life. You are the first," the one on my right with the dark powers took my hand again, "and only."

"That's what you meant by me trusting you."

Somehow, in the last few days, I had taken on the title of supreme secret keeper.

He smiled, glad I understood, and kept my hand in his. I reached over and took the hand of his other half on my left. The rush of each of their powers crawling up me together was intense and delightful and incredibly complimentary, like chocolate-covered strawberries.

"I'd like to give you separate names to keep you straight in my head, otherwise I might go insane. Is that ok?"

"Of course. You may call us whatever you'd like, Sugar," said the one on my left.

"You," I turned to face the one on my right, "are Devil."

I earned a wicked smile full of promises for the name.

"And you," I turned to my left, "are Angel."

He laughed and kissed my cheek.

"Are you always twin brothers on Earth?"

"No," Devil responded. "Sometimes, we are husband and wife. Sometimes sisters or brothers. This time, we are twins. But once, long ago," he gestured towards my head, "we were like you. Trapped together for a while."

I sat forward. Revati and I were both paying attention to what he said next.

"I was the one trapped in his head, with no control over the body," Angel stated in his quiet manner.

"And I was one with the control and the constant nag in my head," Devil said, with a tone of empathy for me.

"So that's how you knew about her," I mused.

"It's written all over your face, Sugar."

It saddened me to hear this. I had thought I was doing a pretty good job of hiding it.

"It's ok. We are keenly observant. It's not obvious to anyone else."

"I don't care if they know, we have been tricked! They are sneaky… man hussies!" Revati scolded.

I rolled my eyes.

"What does she say?" Angel asked.

"She says you are man hussies," I admitted.

Both Devil and Angel started laughing. It was infectious, and I laughed too.

"Wow, that's... the first time I've ever repeated anything Revati said," I admitted.

I felt a bit lighter already, having someone to share my secret with. And Revati seemed pleased too. Something dawned on me, and I sat up a little straighter.

"Wait...you said 'for a while'. Does that mean you figured out how to get into separate bodies?"

They both nodded and smiled in unison. Hope flared in my chest.

"It's not easy, but it is possible," Angel said.

If I hadn't been sitting, I think I would have fallen to my knees in thankfulness. There was a way out of this. Revati was celebrating too.

"Ok, what do we have to do? When can we start?" I pulled my hands away from them and wrung them in anticipation.

"Slow down, Sugar. It takes a lot of preparation and a dangerous journey deep into the Shadowlands. Everything has to be precisely in order. Otherwise, the Shadow People won't allow it. You only get one shot. And if they say no, that's it." Devil explained.

I stood up, and paced back and forth in the room, my mind whirring. The new feeling of hope began to sink some, but I mentally grasped at it. At least it was something.

"Tell them we will start preparing NOW!" Revati yelled at me.

Please be patient. If it's our only chance, we don't want to fuck it up!

"Don't curse at me! Your vulgarness is appalling!"

She yelled some more. I shut my eyes tight against her insults. The hope of getting rid of her had somehow made her voice seem louder and harsher.

Angel and Devil had both gotten up off the sofa and were standing close to me, concerned. A look passed between them, and Devil left the room. Angel wrapped his arms around me into a soothing embrace.

"Sugar, we will get you both free, I promise. But first, we need to take down the bastards selling Echidna's blood."

With the wedding, I had actually forgotten the purpose of it all for a moment, and now it all came back with a vengeance, especially since Revati's hopes, and my own on some level, if I was being honest with myself, were dashed that it wasn't somehow a ploy for Ram to be with us.

As if he could feel my fresh round of concern, he squeezed me tighter.

"Why me? And..how did you choose me? I don't know anything about being a secret agent."

I mumbled into his chest. He smelled so good, and his power was beginning to relax me.

He smiled and pulled back to look into my face.

"We know you don't. That's why you're perfect. We'll train you, sugar. You'll be the best damned secret agent the High Order has ever seen."

I tried to smile in return. I noticed he didn't answer my question about how they had found me in the first place. I was just about to ask again when Revati interrupted me.

"What about me? I don't want to be a secret agent!" Revati yelled.

"Revati says she doesn't want to be an agent."

"Too bad," Devil said, striding into the room, holding his hand palm up.

Something was sitting on his pointer finger. A tiny pink dot.

"She doesn't get to decide. Only you do, Sugar."

"What is that?" I gestured to his finger.

He smiled. He stood in front of me, Angel moving to stand directly behind me.

"Our first wedding gift to you."

"Do NOT trust them!" Revati cried.

"This is iboga," Angel murmured in my ear. His breath tickled.

"What will it do?"

I tried to keep my voice low, but Revati was still yelling at me, so it probably came out a little louder than I intended.

"It's a bit of a... mental vacation from each other, perfectly safe. You'll be back together again soon."

"I don't understand," I said.

I didn't appreciate her yelling, but Revati was right that it was stupid to take drugs from strangers—or husbands? Husband strangers? At least without knowing what they did first.

"It will take her to the edges of the Shadowland," Angel explained.

"The effects will last about eight hours or so. It won't hurt her. It is just blackness there. Very boring. But she will have her own body back for a bit."

"My own body back? Are you lying? What if they are lying? They already tricked us once!"

"Open your mouth, sugar," Devil smiled again.

He was so good at that mischievous smirk. It did wicked things to my insides. I steeled my nerves and did as he asked. He placed the pink dot on my tongue. It was bitter but dissolved rapidly. I made a face at the bitterness.

"What is happening!? Why is it getting dark?! I don't like this..."

Revati's voice was getting quieter and quieter, and then... silence.

I breathed out.

"She's—gone!"

I teared up. It was an incredible feeling, but I wasn't a total monster. I did hope she really was safe.

"You're sure she's ok?"

"Promise, you'll see. She'll be back in the morning." Angel said.

"Come," Devil said, taking my hand and pulling me along.

"I'll show you where the shower is, so you can clean up and unpack."

"And I'll order dinner for us. Vegan tacos ok?" Angel smiled.

His smile wasn't quite as mischievous, but it was every bit as sexy.

I went to ask how he knew I was vegan, but he cut me off, placing his finger against my lips. "Lucky guess. See you in a bit, Sugar."

He slowly slid his finger down, pulling my lip slightly down with it while he stared intently at my mouth. Perhaps Angel wasn't quite the right name for him after all.

Devil cleared his throat, and Angel winked and turned away to use their phone. Devil walked me through to the primary bedroom, featuring the biggest bed I'd ever seen. I noticed my bag at the foot of the bed. He gestured to the open door of the en suite bathroom with a walk-in shower.

"Take all the time you'd like. We'll be waiting downstairs for you."

"For dinner?" I asked, appreciating the complete absence of internal commentary.

He gave me the sexiest smirk yet.

"And anything else you want to happen. It's our wedding night, sugar. We aim to make it memorable if it pleases you."

He slowly grazed his lips across my cheek, stopping before he reached my mouth. His hands found the zipper on the back of my dress. He slowly unzipped it and then backed away, giving me one last look full of lusty intentions before he walked away and went downstairs.

Ooooh.

I was light-headed again, but this time, I wasn't sure if it was hunger, anticipation, fear, or iboga, or what. I had a lot to figure out, and I finally had the available headspace to think.

As the hot water of the shower melted the hairspray and grime away, I keenly felt the absence of Revati. I was alone with my thoughts for the first time since the morning 6 months ago, when I woke up in Ram's bed, listening to the sound of her weeping.

I still had told no one about the voice in my head, not even dear sweet Paul and Stewie, despite her justifiable anger and rage that I should do so. I knew it was wrong, and I felt bad for her. I did! But I was only human, and I was afraid.

Revati was a "Lost", a god who had used a magic potion, eternally trapping their soul inside a human one. The act supposedly made gods completely inactive and without memories or thoughts. It was considered suicide in this new supernatural world I lived in now.

However, in her case, she was a Lost through deception. She had been trying to find Ram and had accidentally bound herself in the process, thanks to Zach, the horrid god who lied to her. He was the same god who not-so-coincidentally ended my life as Chuli Davis as well.

Precious little was known about the Lost on Earth. As far as I knew, I was the only human host that had triggered one awake. I was completely unsure of what would happen to my own soul if the High Order started tinkering with me to free Revati.

The gods I'd met so far treated death on Earth as a casual thing, kind of like going back home after a nice long vacation, since their souls were guaranteed a flight back Upstairs. As a human, I didn't have that luxury. Paul seemed to think human souls got wiped clean and recycled back here to Earth again, but he wasn't entirely certain.

I was still only 28 years old. Despite the trauma I had endured so far this year, and this crazy current situation I found myself in, I didn't have a death wish, and I didn't want to be recycled. But for all I knew, the High Order would kill me just to see what would happen. An agent like Agent Webber could easily snap me in half with his bare hands.

I begrudgingly admitted to myself a less urgent and selfish reason I kept Revati a secret: Spite. Revati was full of opinions and insults, and not afraid to share all of them with me, regardless of my feelings. Granted, I was the only person she's been able to communicate with for centuries, so I couldn't blame her for her lack of manners, but it didn't exactly make me eager to be her best friend. And she HATED that Ram and I had feelings for each other, though, at this point, it was obvious that was past tense.

Now that Revati was on some kind of Shadowland vacation, I took one selfish moment to really think about my own past involvement with Ram. I had grown to care for him, and I had thought a relationship might have worked between us. But apparently, he only used me as some kind of sexual vessel to allow himself to say goodbye to his wife.

The moment had felt so right, but I understood why Revati cried every morning. He had left his wedding ring on the nightstand. And since they (we? It was so confusing to sort) were no longer magically or universally married Upstairs style, that must have been his way of cutting all their ties, saying goodbye forever.

Despite his departure, I kept the ring close to me anyway, on a chain around my neck, even now. I took my soapy hands and caressed it. As I did so, I noticed the gems on my new set of rings and pulled them closer to admire them. One set was lighter gemstones, the other darker. I had initially thought one was a diamond and assumed it was an engagement ring, but now that I was married to not one, but two strangers, I realized the symbolism. I wished I knew more about gemstones. I'd have to ask my husbands what these were.

Panic started to set in again, and I closed my eyes as my heart sped up.

What am I doing?

The enormity of my decision, mostly made with very little thinking and a whole lot of insistence from Revati, bubbled up. I had married two strangers. I was in Las Vegas. I was going undercover to stop a drug cartel from using an illegal creature to poison gods.

Since my world had been completely turned upside down the night of New Year's, I didn't know how to trust anyone, including myself. My internal radar had been so off with Zach that I didn't even think my own instincts were reliable. Of course, I trusted Paul & Stewie as my friends, but there were certain things they kept from me, like Stewie's complete unwillingness to talk about his past and why he was always so alarmed when the High Order was around. My instinct was to not tell them about Revati too, which I didn't quite understand, but it just didn't feel right. I didn't want to get them any more involved in my mess. Now, here in this new crazy situation, Devil & Angel gave me their trust and a secret that could probably get them killed.

Living cautiously since New Year's had gotten me nowhere. Waiting for Ram had gotten me nowhere. I was so very, very, tired of having no one but the voice in my head. I was here now, with two very sexy men who were eager to give me a memorable night. *Can I do this? Can I let them in and allow myself to truly trust again?*

I resolved it was the only solution. I was going to try it their way.

I shut the water off, wrapped myself in a fluffy towel, and wrapped another around my head.

I went out and opened my rolling suitcase. Everything I owned fit neatly inside. There were only a few outfits, most of them just practical clothing choices. I chose a simple sundress with a button front and spaghetti straps. It was the nicest thing I had besides the dress from Armagodden. I brushed my teeth, blotted some more water out of my hair, hung the towels and the wedding dress I'd have to return tomorrow, and headed to the kitchen.

———

Dinner was delicious. We mostly ate in silence. Beautiful, sweet, blessed silence.

I had many questions, but I decided they could all wait since Revati would want to know the answers too. For now, I just did my best to focus on the present moment. I wanted to enjoy every bite, every flavor, and every sensation in my body. I would occasionally glance up at Devil and Angel. They seemed to have some kind of silent conversation with their eyes.

"Can you talk to each other like that?" I finally asked.

"Mmmm… it's more feeling based. Not words, so words are.. not adequate to describe it," Angel tried to explain.

Devil leaned over and lightly traced the thin X-shaped scar on my chest. "It is a lot like Upstairs marriage, that feeling of connection. But perhaps a little stronger. If we lost it, we would be… destroyed."

He looked at me with pity, then stood up and began clearing our plates.

"This... I didn't have that, at least I don't think I did. When it.." I swallowed hard and braced myself. "I felt something in the divorce, but…"

I thought back to how my body bucked and feelings swirled magically about, but I was also so messed up on Veruni that I didn't know what I was feeling.

I remembered the look of utter brokenness and devastation on Ram's broken and bleeding face.

No wonder he left.

Instead of taking the plates to the sink, Devil set them back down on the table and leaned down to me instead, kissing the top of my head.

"Let's not talk of endings anymore. Especially at our beginning, Sugar." He took my hand, the one with the wedding bands on it, and pulled the dark one free.

"I didn't get a chance to say my vows. Come," he commanded, pulling me up and back into the living room.

Angel followed behind.

"How did it go again?" Devil asked.

Angel stood just behind me again, like he did when they had fed me the iboga.

"Do you, Pierre, promise to love, cherish, and obey.."

He whispered in my ear. Devil was right in front of me, intently staring into my eyes just as Angel had done at the wedding. But this time, there were no obnoxious Elvis songs, just the sound of our breathing. Mine became shallow as I felt their powers creeping into me again at their light touches.

"Love… cherish… obey…" Devil whispered while dragging his lips down across my cheek and to the hollow of my neck.

"I do," he said while looking me straight into my eyes to prove his sincerity.

"And do you, Sugar, promise to love, cherish, and obey?"

Angel whispered in my other ear this time, allowing his lips to brush against that side of my neck. Pleasure now assaulted me on all sides.

"I do," I whispered, licking my lips.

Devil pulled back a little, then took my face in both his hands. He said something in French, or maybe some other language. Words didn't matter anymore. He placed his lips on mine, and his dark power poured into my mouth along with his tongue.

Oh yes.

I didn't want to think about trust anymore. I didn't want to think about anything.

"That's it, Sugar, let go," Angel said, kissing my neck.

Devil pulled back, allowing Angel's power to ripple in, replacing the pain and wickedness with sweetness. Dark and light each took turns swirling inside me. It felt incredible. Working in perfect tandem, they opened the buttons of my dress and pulled the straps down over my shoulders until my dress fell to the floor, and I stood in nothing but my panties. They both stepped back a moment, apparently to admire what they had accomplished. I turned around, so I was now facing Angel.

Emboldened by the desire I saw spiking through him, I dove for him, grabbed his face in my hands, and lightly bit his lip, demanding entrance. He obliged, and I sent my tongue crashing into his, our kiss fierce and carnal. I pulled back just a bit while my hands reached around and tried to unbutton his shirt. Thankfully, he had lost the jacket already, but there were still too many clothes on him.

"This-get this off," I grumbled, my hands still fumbling with the buttons.

Devil laughed, and still behind me, he pressed his own now shirtless body against mine and pulled me backward, kissing my shoulder.

"Patience, Sugar, hold still," he said as his hands slid across my stomach, down a little lower, holding me in place.

I stood as still as I could, and watched, eyes hooded

with desire, as Angel undid the buttons and tossed his shirt.

"More," I demanded.

I wasn't sure where this dominance was coming from, but judging from the way his eyes flared as he undid his belt and his fly and stepped out of his pants, I think he liked it. He stood before me in nothing but boxer briefs, his erection obvious. He was sinuous and slinky and looked like sex on legs.

I felt the rough denim of Devil's jeans against the backs of my legs, a contrast to all the hot, soft skin-on-skin felt on my back. I wanted to see him, too.

"Now yours," I practically panted as his fingertips had just begun to dip inside my panties, and I forced myself to step away from him.

It was easy enough to do since Angel was right there to grab me. He turned me around so I could watch as Devil's pants dropped. Devil stalked toward me as if to show me that although he was humoring my demands, he would be the one in charge now. He pulled me away from Angel, wrapping his arms around my waist, and lifted me up, forcing me to wrap my legs around him for balance. Angel still held my upper body aloft, and he was kissing down my shoulder towards my breast. I let out a moan as his mouth reached my nipple at the same time Devil shifted us so his erection rubbed along my underwear.

"Don't stop, oh gods…" I mumbled.

Somehow, they got us to the bedroom. In a flurry of hands and teeth, we were now all naked. I lost track of who was who, but since they were the same, it didn't even matter. Only this dark and light power and ecstasy existed now.

"Are you ready, Sugar?" One of them whispered.

"Yes, oh gods, yes.." I whined, now so worked up into a frenzy of need I forgot anything else.

I felt the divine dark power behind me as I laid back against Devil, his erection pressed against my back. He gripped my thighs and spread them wide, and as I watched in the low light, Angel crept forward on the bed. He smiled a wicked smile, and slowly, slowly ran the head of his erection along my seam, making me shudder and cry out, but Devil held me still. After what felt like a lifetime, he plunged into me.

I nearly blacked out from the feeling, but Devil bit my shoulder, bringing me back from the brink. Angel plundered again and again, and I saw stars as my first orgasm ripped through me. But they weren't ready to let me rest yet. Devil let go, and I was now in Angel's arms. We fell backward, and I rode him for a few more blessed moments before he found his own release.

"My turn," Devil said, as he put me on all fours and entered me from behind, my own need building again, as I scrambled for something to hold on to. It wound up being Angel's shoulders, and he kissed me sweetly, a sharp contrast to the pounding I was taking. I lost myself again in an even deeper, more mind-blowing orgasm as Devil cried out something in an unfamiliar language, or maybe gibberish, and gripped me hard as he finished.

We all collapsed in a puddle of tangled sheets and limbs on the bed, me half on top of Angel, with Devil spooning me from behind. I felt more relaxed than I had in years, though I wasn't sure if it was from sex itself, or because I could finally let go of some of my troubles now that I had someone I trusted. I'm sure being Revati-free for a few more hours helped too. Intro—both of them—had my back. I happily passed out. Memorable wedding night indeed.

six

. . .

THE REST of the week was a whirlwind of training for the upcoming mission. Agent Webber had told me that the cartel was right here in Vegas. It made sense. What better place to set up a drug ring than in a town known for partying? They had some kind of connection at Caesar's Palace, one of the major casino hotels along the strip. Once a month, Introspection was the guest DJ and hotel guest for two nights, usually a Friday and Saturday. That same weekend, the cartel met monthly for some kind of drug lord meeting.

The cartel hired Introspection for his uncanny ability to spot the truth from lies. His presence was required anytime someone new tried to make a deal with them. Within minutes, sometimes even seconds, he routed out anyone with sinister intentions, including several potential undercover High Order agents.

I asked Devil how their power worked. He said it was difficult to explain, but tried.

"When we touch someone, it's as if their feelings and intentions bubble to the surface. With the cartel, it's very easy to tell if someone is very nervous, desperate, or trying to sell something fake. Undercover High Order agents are the worst. They have this smugness about them. They're always the most surprised when I call them out." He laughed.

"Paul calls them sanctimonious bastards," I told him. He laughed even more and agreed.

Angel felt far less comfortable overall around the cartel, so he rarely filled in for Devil for this particular job. I suspected he was the driving force behind notifying the High Order when something particularly bad was about to hit the streets. No one, not the High Order or the cartel, knew about Angel, or that Nevada was Introspection's true home base—no one except for me, and I planned to keep it secret. He had gigs at festivals and nightclubs year-round all over the world, so it was easy to keep his home base unknown. The two of them took turns traveling, which made it much easier to avoid burnout. I thought the idea of a secret twin who could fill in for you when you just wanted to stay home in pajamas sounded amazing.

Sticking with the truth about my identity was going to be essential for this to work, since the cartel had deep connections and could route out my identity at the drop of a hat. The plan was for me to pose as Introspection's naïve new party wife and attend all the functions with him this weekend. I was already pretty good at acting, and since Revati broke through after my night of passion with Ram, hiding my emotions was something I practiced frequently, so I wasn't particularly worried about this part. I had no prior history of working for the High Order, and what would they care about some sad Lost god who wandered around New York City? Even if they miraculously dug up my entire history, they would just know that the High Order issued me a new identity when I was believed to have been killed in a house fire.

I needed to collect DNA evidence from both Echidna

and the god they called Pete. He was the one who gave the snake packets to Star and her boyfriend. He was a "jumper", or a god that jumped to Earth through a portal not controlled by the High Order. Most of the cartel members had initially come through High Order controlled portals, so their identities were already registered, confirmed, and linked to various crimes.

I had heard the basics about jumping from Paul, but Angel & Devil explained it to me in detail, because it was how they always returned to Earth avoiding High Order detection. It meant that your soul was randomly assigned a human avatar somehow, and you would be born in the geographical region that matched your Upstairs origin country, but you had no control over what you could look like or who you could be born to. That's how they had wound up in so many different configurations here on Earth before.

It also circumvented the High Order's registration system, so they had no way of properly identifying someone's origins. I needed something with Pete's DNA so they could properly identify him.

If this mission went right, I would gather enough physical evidence to remove the entire cartel from Earth. If it failed, no one knew when the next opportunity would come again.

I was determined to make sure I didn't fail.

Angel & Devil had a mutual goal of bringing my subterfuge to another level. They both wanted to teach me how to be the best agent I could be, but I strongly doubted their methods were the same training a typical High Order agent would go through.

I was going into a wasp nest of old-school misogyny, so I was going to play the stereotypical dumb trophy wife to fly under their radar and use that weakness against them.

Step one on this path was adjusting my looks, and

Angel was my first escort about town. We went to several shops to find some dresses and corresponding shoes. The only appropriate dress I had was the one I'd worn at Armagodden, so I needed at least a few more club outfits.

I let Revati take the lead for once. I didn't know anything about dressing in a graceful, feminine, and sexy style. She was far better than I was at choosing flattering cuts and colors. Yes, I was showing far more skin than she was comfortable with, but Angel assured us both that it was typical here in the desert. From the flare of approval in his eye, I was sure we were on the right path.

Shoes proved a bit trickier. I wound up with a few platform heels and lace-up bootie-type shoes in the end, but I had to try on many to make sure I could still walk properly and none were too tall, since I had very little practice walking in heels.

Up next was a trip to a high-end salon for a proper trim, along with the products and styling tips to keep my hair looking good. After that, we went to a makeup store where I received a makeover and bought a bunch of random makeup supplies, including waterproof mascara that didn't run.

When my look was complete, I hardly recognized myself. Naoma was a stranger, which was just fine for this role, anyway.

Revati seemed to be slowly coming around and enjoying herself after her initial disappointment and heartbreak over the wedding. I suspected part of it was because someone other than just me finally acknowledged her. Angel was especially sympathetic to her plight, having been in the same situation himself, and he made sure to include her and ask her opinion on things.

The other reason she was most likely working on her attitude was that she did not enjoy her trip to the Shadowlands very much, and I now had the power to send her back any time I chose. My wedding gift included a bottle with several of the little dots of iboga. I didn't enjoy holding a threat over her, but it was nice to finally have some kind of leverage over her. Whenever she would start yelling at me, all I had to do was finger the bottle I kept in my bag, and she would quiet herself.

What she didn't know was that while she was away, Angel and Devil had explained to me that iboga was not something to toy with. Apparently, the withdrawal effects got nastier with each trip, and if I took it too many times in a row, I risked getting sucked into the Shadowlands myself.

While I was eventually going to go there so we could get Revati in a different body, they insisted it required rituals and preparations that we would focus on later, after we closed this current case and got Echidna's DNA for the High Order. But I kept all those thoughts as buried as I could, so Revati couldn't snatch onto them.

Devil was especially good at distracting me enough to keep all my thoughts and questions and concerns at bay. He took me out night after night to different bars and clubs and even magic shows. He thought it was essential that I learn some pickpocketing techniques, of all things.

"You see, Sugar, it's the ultimate art of distraction. If you can pickpocket, you can get anything you need this weekend," he said next to my ear to me one night at a crowded bar.

After some tips and suggestions and several more drinks, I was ready to try it.

"Stupid girl, what are you doing!? What if you get arrested!?"

I'm not keeping anything! He's right, it's good practice!

"I still don't trust him. Angel is ok, but Devil's just..."

He's fine! It's all fine! Can you please be quiet so I can train?

Revati scoffed. "Yeah, if you call drinking every night and now stealing proper *training*."

I ignored that last sting and scoped the scene, looking for an easy victim at the bar. I spotted a man who had just paid for his beer and then put his wallet back in his back pocket.

I slid off my bar stool and felt quite tall in my strappy new platform heels. I was wearing a short, tight, and very low-cut dress, and I adjusted it to make sure nothing was showing. I caught up with him just as he was walking away from the bar.

"Jim! Hey!" I said and grabbed his arm, the one that was holding the beer.

I tugged on it just enough that his very full beer spilled down the front of him. He looked shocked and confused.

"Oh my gosh, I am SO Sorry! I thought you were my friend, and now I've spilled your beer!"

I took my hand and stroked down his chest where the beer had spilled, as if I could somehow wipe it off with my bare hand. He looked at my hand, and then at the rest of me. His eyes widened.

"It's ok.." he said, trailing off as he noticed just how low cut my dress was.

"Are you sure? Oh gosh, I feel so awful!" I said as I continued to keep my hand on his chest with just enough pressure that he didn't notice the feel of his wallet coming out of his pocket and into my hand. Once I had it secure, I patted his chest again and took my hand away.

"Well, you're a proper gentleman then. So sorry again! Oh, there he is! Jim!"

I pretended to wave to someone in the near distance and lost myself in the crowd so he couldn't see me anymore.

"Amazing, Sugar! You're a natural!" Devil laughed and kissed me when I made it back to him, then handed me another gin & tonic he'd ordered me while I was away playing pickpocket.

I didn't know whether I should be horrified or proud of myself as I felt the wallet in my hand. I took a sip of my drink and then got the bartender's attention.

"Excuse me, I found this on the ground. I think maybe someone dropped it?"

I handed the wallet over and hoped its owner thought to ask the bartender if anyone had turned it in when he realized it was missing.

Later that same evening, I was about to suggest we turn in for the night—well, technically, morning—when Devil spoke.

"I think you're ready for one final lesson, Sugar."

"What kind of a lesson this time? Breaking and entering?" Revati asked.

Oh, come on, knock it off.

"What's she saying?" Devil asked.

"Nothing important. What kind of lesson?" I asked.

A slow smile spread across Devil's face. "Dancing."

This confused me. "But I thought you liked my dancing, and I was already good at it?"

I had figured out on my own that I could project sexuality with my dance moves. Revati insisted this wasn't a power of hers from Upstairs, so it must be my own particular special goddess power. Before she was Lost, she hadn't been on Earth since her very first life, and she certainly hadn't been trying to dance provocatively back in the day when her father, King Kakudmi, was searching for the ideal husband for her.

None of us quite understood what the relationship between a Lost and an Earth host like me was. If I could finally get her out, did that mean I would lose all my goddess status and power? Would I just be an ordinary human? Probably. I tried not to think about it and instead focused on harnessing that little bit of power while I still had it. Devil's hand on my arm pulled me back to the present.

"Oh I do, and you are. But I want you to be the *best*. I want you to be irresistible. You'll see."

Before I could argue, he pulled me into a different kind of bar than the ones we'd be partying at. A topless one.

Lots of red lights and poles graced the many stages arranged throughout the space. Devil guided me to a table near an empty stage. A beautiful, barely clad young woman took our order. She looked to be in her early 20s, and she had long blonde hair and a pretty smile. She returned with our drinks just before a performer came out and began dancing, starting with undulating around near a table a few down from ours.

I had never been to a strip club before, and I felt pretty weird watching someone wearing nothing but a tiny pair of undies. I kept wanting to divert my eyes—it felt voyeuristic. Devil leaned in.

"Hey, it's ok, you're supposed to watch, Sugar. That's the point. She wants you to. Check out their reactions to her, too. Which moves do they like the best? Why?"

As the night rolled on, Devil guided me around the club to watch various dancers perform. Sometimes for others, sometimes directly in front of us. I got progressively more comfortable with the situation and better at noticing which moves were better received than others, and who was a better dancer and why.

"Ok, time for Phase Two," Devil smiled and approached the staff.

They escorted us to a private room, and the dancer we had both agreed was the best sauntered in from a different door.

"A 30 minute private lesson, Sugar," Devil said, smiling.

I was a little nervous, but the woman, a tall redhead named Amanda, turned out to be very sweet, and absolutely willing to show me her particular dance moves and guide me through them, sometimes dancing directly with me. I had never been the straightest arrow in the quiver, but my sexual experiences with women were limited to a few dates and kisses in my late teens and early twenties. Just like with men, I had never really seemed to find the right person.

This woman was the perfect amount of sex mixed with professionalism to show me everything I needed to know. Ultimately, I wound up getting a lap dance so she could show me just how erotic you could be when someone was still sitting down. I had to admit, it turned me on quite a bit. I was drunk enough, and the music was loud enough that I could tune out Revati's protests about what marriage should and shouldn't be. But I recalled our recent vows, and they did not mention fidelity at all. Besides, Devil seemed absolutely on board with what was happening—it had been his idea, after all.

We switched places, and now it was my turn to try the lap dance moves. Somehow I wound up with my dress pulled down to my waist, the three of us trading kisses and touches until our time was up, and Devil put me back together and brought me home to bed.

———

I might have been on a path of poor life choices this week, but it was the most fun I'd had in forever, so I was rolling with it, and I felt pretty confident in my secret agent abilities by the time we were ready to go undercover.

I truly enjoyed getting to know both Angel and Devil and seeing how they worked. Especially when that work involved taking my body to new heights of pleasure. It was a skill they were both incredibly talented at, either working together, as they had on our absolute mind-blowing wedding night, or separately, stealing kisses and intimate moments in discreet corners all over the city. Were we in love? Absolutely not. But that didn't mean it wasn't a good time, and it was nice to take a break from being cautious all the time. I could get as crazy and wild as I wanted, especially with Devil, who seemed to bring that side out of me more than anyone. It didn't matter if I was drunk out of my mind or heavily flirting and stealing little trinkets from tourists; I knew I could trust him to get me out of the situation and back home again.

———

Thursday night was our last night out on the town before the mission officially began, and Intro invited Agent Webber to go over the last-minute details. Our meeting spot was a dart bar called Flight Club. We entered the Canal Shoppes by the Venetian, one of the more outlandish resorts. It was designed to feel like Venice, Italy. I'd never been to Venice, but I suspected it was not quite like this. The shops had a canal running right through the mall-like area, complete with gondolas cruising the chlorinated water. Above us, it appeared to be daytime, thanks to the ceiling, designed to look like a sunny day with wispy clouds.

Eventually, we got to the bar. It featured a series of semi-private areas, each with its own dart board, area for food and drinks, and a tall, upholstered booth-like bench for sitting. It was both entirely public, yet also secluded. We checked in, headed to our reserved spot, and ordered our first round of drinks. We finished ordering the few vegan options on the menu just as Webber approached. He was wearing regular pants of some kind. I've never been very good at identifying the style types of men's pants, other than to say they were dark, not military, and not jeans. On top, he wore a classic white linen button-down shirt, the top button open, and a pair of mirrored aviator sunglasses.The transformation was surprising. If he wasn't so large, I'm not sure I would have recognized him. He didn't look as threatening this way, and he fit right in with the rest of the tourists and locals.

"Don't be fooled girl, you know he still has weapons galore under that shirt," Revati said.

Probably.

He took off his sunglasses in the much dimmer atmosphere of our corner. I couldn't figure out the look on his face. He looked possibly annoyed, possibly pained, or maybe both. Maybe the glaring lights out on the strip bothered him, too.

"Webber, so glad you could make it! You like the place? I would have loved to meet you at the Appian Way shops instead—have you seen their statues of the Gods? Quite entertaining. The Fall of Atlantis fountain show is particularly fascinating if you've never seen it. I didn't want to risk you turning up on Caesar's security cameras, so here will have to do."

Devil smirked. He seemed a little too eager to taunt Webber. Instead of losing his cool, Agent Webber was entirely straight-faced as he replied.

"We throwing darts or words, *moitié pourrie*?"

I looked at Devil, and he looked a little surprised and a little impressed. I was pretty sure veiled threats and secrets were being volleyed about, but the server came with our drinks, and the mood shifted.

I decided I wanted the work part of this done as quickly as possible, so I spoke up.

"Can we go over this DNA thing again? What exactly do you need? Hair? Saliva?"

"In a perfect world, they'd like both, Ms..."

Webber was about to call me Ms. Bhatt but then stopped, probably unsure of what I wanted to be called now that I was married.

"Naoma will do," I smiled at him.

Ms. Bhatt was too formal anyway. He didn't respond to that.

"Your turn, Sugar," Devil walked back over to me from the line and handed me a dart.

I looked at where his dart had stuck. It was stuck in the second ring from the center. Pretty darn good for the first throw of the night.

Mine hit the target, but near the outside; not anywhere close to the bullseye, but not in the cork circle surrounding the board either. Webber stepped up to take his turn. He hardly seemed to look at it. One second, the dart was in his hand, the next, it was dead center in the bullseye.

Damn.

I was very glad he was on my side and not planning on aiming anything at me.

The details of the mission continued. We went over a list of drop points along the strip near Caesar's Palace. There were no High Order agents in the resort. It was too risky. There were, however, several installed in other nearby areas, and each drop-off point would be regularly monitored for the duration of the mission.

After a few more rounds of drinks, food, and darts, I was still trying to get the hang of dart throwing. My aim was decent, but I wasn't fully consistent. Devil was very good, hitting either the bullseye or darn close to it nearly every time. But Webber was incredible. His dart went precisely dead center of anywhere he wanted it to go. I stood parallel to him and watched him closely to figure out what he was doing, but it was no use. He was too fast.

"Shoot, how the heck do you DO that?" I asked, practically whining.

He cocked an eyebrow, but didn't elaborate.

"Seriously, can you show me? Please?"

He barked out one word. "No."

Devil laughed. "Come on, Webber, give her a lesson."

Agent Webber glared at him. "I don't take orders from you."

Devil didn't let his intimidating stare affect him.

"Yes, you only take orders from Those Who Judge. I'm well aware. But you DO take tips from me," he smiled and leaned in a little conspiratorially.

"And here's an important one. Pleasing her is a very rewarding pastime." He strolled over to me and put his hand on my hip.

"Don't worry, sugar, I'll give you a tip and then some," he seemed quite confident that his double meaning was understood as he nuzzled against my neck, planting a kiss in the hollow just below my ear before he raised his head again and spoke.

"Go to the oche," he said.

"The what?"

I was partly aroused, and partly embarrassed at what that conversation and kiss might have looked like, so it took me a moment to come to my senses.

"The line. It's called an oche in darts," he spoke in that soft, sweet tone that I loved.

I moved up to the line.

"It's your stance. Stand like this..."

He placed his hand on my hip and tilted me, his front to my back.

"Good, now hold your arm like this."

He placed the dart in my hand and wrapped his arm around mine, guiding it.

"Now, when you get here," he guided my arm in the correct position, "let go."

He let his hands fall and stepped back. The air felt significantly cooler after his departure, and I closed my eyes for a moment while a wave of goosebumps washed over me and passed again. I took the dart and tried to envision the exact flow of movements we had just enacted together.

Thunk.

It went right in the bullseye.

"Yessss!!!" I yelled, raising my hands and dancing around.

I walked over to Devil, who pulled me in for a kiss. He said something in French, but I had no idea what. Didn't matter, anyway. I kissed him again, a little longer the second time.

"Can you stop? This is public, and this is a work meeting!" Revati yelled at me.

Sorry, not sorry.

Devil laughed. "Guess she didn't need your help after all."

"Good," Agent Webber said.

Just then, the server approached with our dessert—sticks of cotton candy.

"Sugar on a stick, just like you!" Devil said, laughing.

————

At long last, it was Friday afternoon, and we arrived at Caesar's Palace for check-in. This time, however, there was a mix-up at the desk. The room he traditionally booked, an ideal suite near an exit if he ever got in a jam, had been given to another, and half of the casino's rooms were currently being renovated.

The poor young woman at the desk was terrified. Even

though she wasn't a god, it was obvious she knew Intro-spection as the famous DJ, and she felt awful to be the bearer of bad news. Our proximity and Devil's watchful eyes were clearly making her even more nervous and uncomfortable as she frantically searched the computer to find us a suitable room. I wrapped my arm around Devil.

"Why don't we go… explore for a bit?" I asked him as I placed my hand on his chest, then down a little further.

"Then we'll stop back and see where this lovely woman found a room for us?"

The woman looked relieved and readily agreed. Devil smiled at me and kissed the corner of my mouth. To anyone watching, we seemed like a couple eager to find a private corner to devour each other in. But one of our goals was to find clues to identify Echidna properly, and we were eager to find out if she was still here. We may as well get started immediately. Devil took my hand and pulled me toward the casino.

"I know where Pete's office is," he whispered.

Pete was the god I needed evidence from, and he was some kind of manager here. He had an office, but it was on the other side of the casino. We wound our way through the slot machines and the clouds of cigarette smoke created by the guests. It amazed me that smoking was still very much a thing here. The machines were all different and ranged from old-school ones that resembled 1980s alarm clocks to 10-foot-tall digital ones with images of hulking gods in 3D graphics. The combination of all the speakers from each machine, along with the occasional ringing of bells or dramatically loud and long songs when people won, made a terrific cacophony of sound. I wondered what the appeal of this all was, and why so many people were willing to spend so much time and money in casinos.

Finally, we got through to the other side and found the hall with Pete's office door. Devil must've paid attention when he was here in the past, because he easily punched in the code to unlock the door and let us in. There was a desk with a computer and a pile of papers next to it. He pulled me into him for a kiss, and picked me up, placing me on the desk just beside the computer, hitching my already short skirt up even further in the process. I kissed the side of his neck and began running my hands up his body, under his t-shirt. If there were any security cameras, they were getting quite a show. Hopefully, it was enough of one that they wouldn't notice that his left hand was attempting to type a password into the computer to gain access and that my eyes were searching the room for anything that might have recent DNA on it. When my roaming hands dipped even lower, he let out a bit of a groan.

"Sleuthing is much more fun with you, Sugar," he said, then he nipped my ear and went back to scanning the records of the hotel guests for any clues.

"I don't like this one bit! This is scandalous! Whose office is this? What if you get caught?!" Revati was yelling again.

She hated how my senses of caution and propriety had atrophied around Devil, and she took to lecturing me more and more frequently, ignoring my subtle iboga threats. In turn, I was losing all politeness back to her.

Shut up, grandma!

"Oh, you—" she huffed, but we heard voices coming down the hall, and she stopped to listen, more concerned than me.

With hardly any detectable movement, Devil logged out of the computer and put it back in sleep mode. Then he turned his focus entirely to kissing me as a fluorescent light clicked on overhead and the voices stopped in the doorway. Devil turned as if he had only just realized their presence. He was still in front of me, blocking me from view, his hand still wrapped around my bare thigh.

"This room's taken," he said with a smirk. "Turn the light out on your way out," and he went back to kissing me.

"Intro, mate, have a little respect, yeah? This is my office!"

The man had some kind of British-sounding accent. He didn't sound exceptionally upset about the situation, however.

"Take your trollop to your room for that kind of fun."

Devil pulled me up to stand next to him, his arms around me, righting my skirt along the way.

"This, *mate*," he stated with a bite, "is no trollop. This is my beautiful *wife*. And we would be in *our* room, but your incompetent hotel staff has somehow given it to someone else. We are just passing the time while we wait for them to fix it," he said, then dropped a lingering kiss on my cheek.

The man stood silent for a moment, looking me over. He didn't seem to know what to make of this news.

"Hi, I'm Naoma," I said, smiling, and I stepped forward, holding out my hand for him to shake.

"How charming you are, Naoma," he smiled. "I'm Pete."

Pete appeared to be in his late 30s or early 40s, with a lanky build, sandy thinning blonde hair and blue eyes. He curled his long fingers around mine, squeezing them firmly before letting go. He had the kind of smile that promised wicked things, all of them terrible. My insides raged as I recognized him from my vision. This was the man who gave my friends Echidna's blood. I kept my cool, but internally, I promised myself that this fucker was going to pay. I next turned to the man standing behind him in the hall, half blocked by Pete. As Pete stepped aside a bit, I got a look at the man standing behind him.

I was about to raise my hand and introduce myself, but

my voice stuck in my throat and my hand stayed frozen to my side.

"AAAAAAAAAAAHHHHH!!" Revati screamed in both fear and relief.

If I had been the type of person who fainted, I would have. I was, however, the type of person who threw up when overwhelmed, and I stepped back and closed my eyes, nauseous, but determined to fight it.

Devil wrapped his arms around me again and gave me a gentle squeeze, a physical reminder to keep it together at this moment. My thoughts and Revati's voice were both frantic, trying to grasp what was happening in this situation.

Ram is here.

Ram. Is. Here.

seven

. . .

WHEN I DARED to look up again, Ram was staring at Devil. I swore there was a split second where he looked murderous, but as I watched, he smoothed his impassive and guarded mask back on his face, much like he did the first time I met him—in his current human form, anyway.

He was working as an undercover agent, much like I was doing now. He was pretending to be an arrogant IT person at Burning Wind, the beloved publishing house I spent years helping to build before my world was forever altered when I was given Veruni nectar and learned about the world of gods and goddesses regularly visiting Earth. Well, I wouldn't say he was necessarily *pretending* to be arrogant. He was an asshole, and also a very talented IT person.

And he also happened to be the long-lost love and current ex-husband of the Goddess that lived within me, a Goddess that awakened only because of a night of love and passion that rocked me so deep it freed her. I quickly looked away. I had no idea what to do.

"Not this High Order douche again," Devil said, his breath ruffling my hair a bit from where he held me.

"I sent you packing the last time you tried to set us up."

"Well, that's the rub right there, Intro. He claims he no longer works for the High Order." Pete chuckled slightly. "Says he got fired."

"Fired!?" Revati yelled in my head.

I kept silent. I no longer trusted myself to speak about anything at all.

Ram held out his hand to Devil, who stepped forward to grip Ram's hand while studying him closely.

"It's true. He doesn't work for them. He hates them." Devil continued while staring directly at Ram. "So why are you here then, douche?"

"Money." Ram finally spoke. "I have Soma, and I'm willing to sell it for the right price."

Every word that came out of his mouth felt like a punch to the gut.

Like Veruni, Soma was another Hindu nectar. Historical texts said it was intoxicating to the Hindu gods. If he were here, selling it, there must be some truth in that.

"He's lying, he has to be!" Revati cried. "He wouldn't dare get involved with these people!"

"He's really here to negotiate the sale of Soma," Devil said, sounding surprised.

He stared at him for a few more moments, then he shrugged his shoulders towards Pete before continuing.

"He's also feeling rather blindsided at the moment."

"Blindsided? Why?" Pete questioned. "Everyone knows the first step to any deal is to pass the Introspection test. Ram, of all gods, especially knows, since he's tried and failed before."

"True. But the thing is," he paused for a moment, giving me a quick apologetic glance, "he was never expecting to find me married to the reason he lost his job."

Pete barked out a surprised laugh. "Oh, delightful. Please, elaborate."

I stared at Ram, but he wouldn't look at me. The Lost database at the High Order was Ram's magnum opus in this earthly life. If he was fired, he would have lost access to it, as well as any of the High Order's resources. I felt a pang of empathy. That was a feeling I could understand all too well, with all the work I had done at Burning Wind being taken away from me. I had also lost all my earthly belongings, my entire family connection, and even the privacy of my own thoughts.

Wait a minute.

My empathy quickly turned to rage as I realized that with all I had lost, I turned it into a desire to bring down the cartel that allowed all of that to happen.

Meanwhile, here was Ram, who knew what these fuckers had done to me, but instead of fighting them, he was trying to make a quick buck from them after losing, what exactly, besides his job? His manly pride, perhaps? As if he couldn't get money from his movie-star brother. He hadn't ever bothered to check up on me in the slightest after our night together. After consideration, I bet the asshole blamed me for getting fired.

Between my rage and Revati's desperate sobs, I still wasn't willing to elaborate for Pete, especially since I didn't even know Ram had been fired until right now. I looked down at the floor before my anger turned to tears, a very annoying habit I had sometimes.

Devil protected me in his embrace yet again, and I relaxed into him, happy that I had at least one person here I could trust. Ram too remained silent, and it was Devil that finally broke the awkward silence.

"This asshat," he casually spoke to Pete while lightly stroking up and down my arm with the back of his hand," allowed my sweet wife to get kidnapped and nearly killed under his watch. He was such a terrible agent that even HE got kidnapped. Fortunately for him,

Naoma managed to kill the abductor and save both their lives."

Here he turned a cold glare to Ram, "even though he had utterly failed her as an agent."

He paused again for a moment, his expression turning neutral again.

"You can trust him for a little deal like this, Pete, but he's not the man I'd want watching my back if I were ever in a jam."

Pete looked intrigued, and then it was as if an idea struck him. "She's not—"

But whatever he was asking was cut off by Devil.

"It's about time we check to see if our room is ready. See you this evening, Pete. And Ram? Stay the fuck away from my wife. You seem to be dangerous for her to be around."

He guided me past both gods and back to the desk. Our room was indeed ready, and we didn't speak at all until we were safely inside. Devil hugged me fiercely.

"So brave, Sugar. So stoic."

Apparently, he was impressed with how I had been able to hold it together in the face of the agent who had failed me. Funny thing was, I had never once felt like Ram had failed me, at least I hadn't until now. Deep down, I kept hoping he would turn back up with a damn good reason why he never contacted me. I was ready to forgive him. But his dealings with the cartel for a some spending money were absolutely unforgivable.

Now that we were alone, I was free to fall apart like Revati, but I was also afraid that if I started crying, I'd never stop, so I just stood there, screwing my eyes shut, shoving my feelings down as hard as I could.

"You knew all that?" I asked, as he let go of me.

He knew I was referring to his knowledge of what had happened with Ram. We had not discussed my recent past at all. He and Angel both knew it was a painful subject, and each had declined to ask, but they would be pretty remiss in their duties as an agent if they hadn't looked into my history before marrying me.

Devil nodded, then moved his hand forward and unbuttoned my top buttons. His left hand found the long chain that held Ram's ring, while his right pointer finger traced the outline of the sensitive pink scar on my chest from our divorce.

"It's him, isn't it?" he whispered.

I couldn't speak. I just nodded. I barely heard him over Revati's continued sobs.

Will you ever run out of tears?

I internally snapped at her. She was too distraught to notice. Devil dropped the necklace and buttoned my shirt. He sighed.

"For once, I wish it were Angel here with you right now. He would help you through this in a sweet and gentle way. But we can't switch places now, so we're going to do this my way."

He stormed over to the phone. "Room service? One bottle of rye whiskey, room 201, et vite!"

Then he turned back to me.

"Sugar, you get that bottle and you take iboga right now, you hear me? Right now."

He stalked over to me like a predator. I felt his dark power increasing in potency as he approached. His look brooked no nonsense. I opened the bottle, fumbling a little, and pulled out one of the precious pills. Revati still wasn't paying me any attention, lost in her own misery, which happened to be the loudest misery one could ever happen to have. I let it dissolve on my tongue and kept my eyes shut tight. After a few seconds, the volume on Revati had been turned down, but she was still there. I opened my eyes in time to see Devil take a bottle from room service.

Damn, that was quick.

"Is she gone?" He asked, ripping the plastic off a cup and pouring in a substantial amount of whiskey.

I shook my head.

"Another then," he said.

I put one more on my tongue and he handed me the plastic cup of whiskey. It was very thin plastic, tricky not to spill. Angel and Devil had warned me that my body would become tolerant to iboga and I would need more in the future. I gulped down as much of the whiskey as I could, nearly choking. At long last, the crying ceased. I felt oddly quiet and hollow now that Revati was no longer hogging the emotional spotlight in my brain. I felt the warmth and numbing sensation of the whiskey beginning to circulate, and I felt the thoughts of rage and hurt and betrayal lurking in the vacuum that remained.

Before they could get rooted, Devil's dark power slammed into me as he took my arms and pinned me against the wall. I gasped and opened my eyes. It hurt, but it pulled me back to the moment. I looked into Devil's dark eyes. He looked intimidating and ready to devour me.

"Sugar, I'm going to pleasure you until you forget everything but my name."

———

By the time we made it downstairs to the restaurant, I was showered, primped, and dressed to impress. I was wearing one of my new club dresses. It was a slinky, shiny, deep blue marble print bodycon dress with cutouts that exposed vast swaths of my skin. I paired it with the boots and lipstick Stewie helped me pick out before Armagodden. Gods, I missed him & Paul so much. I couldn't wait until this mission was over so I could report back and tell them everything. Well, not everything. Ok, I had no idea what I would, and could, tell them.

"Hi, guys! I'm married and dress like a stripper now, but it's ok because I can dance like one too!"

But I sure did miss them.

Strapped to my waist was my little bag. It didn't go with my outfit, but it was essential to keep supplies on me in case I got a chance to collect any evidence, and I needed the extra boost of security my paring knife gave me.

I was no longer on the verge of a breakdown. True to his words, Devil had provided a very mind-blowing few hours, alternating pleasure and pain to the point where I was screamed out, admittedly sore, and fully sated. It was an unorthodox method for sure, but I certainly wasn't going to complain, and if there were secret cameras or spies, it fit our cover story to a tee.

I still had a few red marks here and there, including what looked suspiciously like a bite mark on my thigh, but I didn't care who saw them.

Assembled at the dinner table was a small gathering of the key cartel players. Seated at the head of the table was Seth Godwin, head of the cartel. Upstairs, he was known as Set, the Egyptian God of harsh deserts, chaos, and foreigners. He was in his 60s in this earth life. He had on a very nice suit, and his short, dark, slicked-back hair was graying at the temples. His nose was a little elongated and curved downward. I was reminded of the hieroglyphic images of him with some kind of aardvark-like head. He had an eerie calmness and a mob boss vibe for sure. Even if they hadn't warned me that he was incredibly dangerous, I would have quickly figured that out on my own. He was terrifying.

Seated next to him was Pete, whom I had already met. Judging from Pete's actions, his job in high management at the casino, and his role as head of logistics for the cartel, they suspected he was a trade or commerce god of some kind.

Seated opposite Pete was Gil, short for Gilfaethwy, a

Welsh god. Background research dug up some wild stories about him, and how he had his brother Gwydion trick their uncle so he could rape his uncle's virginal servant. As punishment, his uncle had turned him and his brother into animals and had them mate with each other. In animal form, he had given birth to three sons: One half-stag, one half-pig, and one half-wolf.

Two of those sons at this table: Hych and Bleid. It was obvious that these three made up the ever-important "dumb muscles" category in the cartel. Both men were bulky and strong with thick necks like their father/mother, but Hych had an upturned nose and ruddy appearance, and Bleid had a sinister-looking grin with far too many teeth. I wondered where their half-stag brother was.

I got the chills as I remembered Agent Webber warning me that some of the cartel members had some nefarious ideas when it came to women. I never, ever wanted to be left alone with any of them. My hand kept sliding down to touch the pocket of my bag that held the knife.

Seated between Pete and Hych was a gorgeous and unreal-looking woman. She didn't speak but glared with golden eyes, casting murderous glances at the gods around her.

Echidna.

As if she heard me call her, she looked up and stared at me before looking down at the table. The host escorted me to my seat at the end, across from Devil, directly next to Ram. I suspected it was Pete's idea of a good time, as he was smirking and looking back and forth between the three of us. I took a deep breath.

Stay calm, you can do this.

I pep-talked myself in the beloved absence of Revati, who wasn't scheduled to arrive back until the wee hours of the morning when the iboga wore off. The silence in the wake of her disappearance did wonders to help me focus on the conversation.

There was a bit of idle chit-chat about trivial matters between Hych and Bleid. The table was candle-lit, and the food was brought out by white-gloved servants. The entire scene reminded me of the obligatory "dinner party" scene present in every regency romance novel I'd ever read, which was quite a few. I had always enjoyed reading about the dukes and earls and their spunky love interests set in London in the early 1800s. I could damn well nearly always guess who the bad guy was, and I loved the guarantee of a happy ending, despite whatever the troubles the couple came across. I rooted for them every time. But as much as the dinner had that feeling, I was certain that no heroine in such a book would have looked like a stripper and slept with more than one of the people at the table. Plus, I was determined to make sure none of these bastards in the cartel lived happily ever after.

Then it occurred to me that any of these gods could have actually been on Earth and participated in just that kind of dinner party in real life. The absurdity of that thought teamed with the excruciating presence of Ram next to me made me burst out with a nervous giggle.

Ram refused to even turn his head in my direction.

I forced myself to stare at him, to try to build up a tolerance for the heartache it caused me. I had been too overwhelmed to catch more than a glance at him as we marched out of the office earlier, but now I studied him. He looked absolutely gorgeous, of course. He had cut his hair, which hung in a shaggy style. It would be a silly haircut on others, but somehow it set off his soft, smooth face perfectly.

I remembered staring at him for the first time, back when I was trying to read his aura in my office. I guessed that it hadn't exactly changed to sunny yellow. This time, instead of seeming open and willing to talk to me, the look in his eyes was cold and hard. He was furious.

"Nice hair. You look like a missing member of the Beatles, back before they got into psychedelics. I'd say they ditched you because of your stance on drugs, but clearly, that's changed."

Apparently, my only defense against his beauty was meanness. I turned back to my admittedly delicious soup. Instead of responding, he acted as if I hadn't even spoken. I had a moment where I wondered if maybe he had lost his hearing during the events in the abandoned mine. He had been beaten very badly, but he seemed to hear me just fine that same night. Had something happened after that? But then he casually handed the salt down the table when someone asked. It appeared he was only deaf to anything I said.

My hands began shaking with hurt and anger. I tried to set down the spoon I was holding, but it clanged to the floor. I doubled over in my chair, sticking my head under the table to find where it had landed and retrieve it. Perhaps it was unladylike, but I needed a break to recover, even if only for a moment. While I was looking for the spoon, something else caught my eye. On Echidna's ankle, I spotted some kind of ankle monitor peeking out from under the cuff of her pants. *Are they tracking her movements, or somehow forcing her to comply? Perhaps she isn't a willing participant in any of this.*

This new information gave me the fortitude I needed to get back to the mission. I got off my chair and crawled further under the table to get a better look at the device. Fortunately, my spoon gave me the perfect cover, as it had slid just out of my reach.

As if she knew what I was doing, Echidna crossed her ankles, allowing her cuff to ride up just a little further. Now that I got a better look, I grabbed my spoon and crawled back out.

Unfortunately, I chose to crawl out next to my chair on the side closest to Ram. His scent filled my nose as I got up and returned to my seat. I closed my eyes for just a moment, remembering how much I had always loved his smell. When I opened them again, all eyes were staring at me, including the serving staff standing by.

"I was… my spoon," I held out the spoon in my hand as if it were somehow the answer to my entire lack of manners.

A server silently approached, slid the dirty spoon out of my hand, then removed my soup in preparation for the main meal, even though I had hardly eaten any. The awkward silence was punctuated by Devil.

"You know I love you on all fours," he laughed and gave me a twinkling and appreciative smile.

I suspected he was trying to make everyone there feel as uncomfortable as I felt. There was also a hint of a question in his eyes. He knew I had discovered some kind of intel.

Mr. Godwin cleared his throat as if he was determined to bring civility back to the table with some more polite small talk.

"Who is your father, madam, and what is his occupation?"

I fought back the urge to laugh.

Madam? My father's profession?

This truly felt like a centuries-old conversation. I doubted Mr. Godwin spent a lot of time dining with strangers. I maintained a polite smile and a demeanor best suited to a lady. Devil reached across the table and grabbed my hand.

"You don't have to talk about it if you don't want to, Sugar."

I smiled at him. It was sweet of him to defend me against these personal questions.

"My father—that is, my stepfather—he was an auto mechanic."

Talking about the man who raised me in this company felt wrong, as if their association could tarnish his memory.

"And your true father?" He prodded, oblivious to my uncomfortableness.

"He was killed in an accident when I was a small child. I did not know him."

A small wave of sadness and regret lapped at me as it always did on the rare occasion I thought of the father I never really knew. I had the vaguest memory of him holding me, of hearing his laughter and knowing he loved me, but I was so young that I couldn't be certain that I wasn't just making it up.

"And you were raised here in America?" He continued the interview as all eyes stayed on me.

I was just about to answer when Devil stood up, pulling me up and out of my seat with him.

"Naoma doesn't need to tell you her history. If you'll excuse us, we have some things we need to catch up on before my set tonight. We'll see you at the club."

We left the dining room, but I made sure I cast apologetic glances around as if I were the obedient wife who had no choice but to listen to her husband.

Pete seemed the most fascinated, as always. When we got to the doorway, I was just about to ask him what all that was about when he pulled me against him and kissed me senseless, as if to demonstrate to the table exactly what we planned to do for the next hour before his set. A mean, vengeful part of me hoped Ram got a very good view of that kiss.

———

Finally, it was club time, and Introspection's music set began. He drove the crowd wild from the DJ booth, an exclusive area above the main crowd, with enough room behind the equipment to house a few tables and most of the cartel. I spent my time dancing around the perimeter, admiring the massive spinning chandelier and light show that dominated the packed space. I was toeing the line between enjoyment and just enough seduction to allow no doubt why Introspection and I had "fallen in love" so quickly.

On the surface, we were perfect for each other: She who had nothing left of her previous life except a love of dancing, and he (well, they) who specialized in driving people crazy by spinning dance music. I thought back to the original agreement- we were married for this earthly life for as long as I would like. Would that be so bad?

Soon, they were going to help me get rid of Revati, and I could live a quiet and perhaps happy existence as Mrs. Introspection. And Revati, in her new body, could go crawling back to her beloved Ram, if he would even bother to look up long enough to notice her presence. I didn't want to examine why that thought rankled me so much. Of course, they were perfect for each other. And I wanted everyone to have a happy ending, didn't I?

After some consideration, I had determined that Ram must hate me so much he had just written me completely out of his life. He couldn't even look at me. His reasons were obvious once I started considering it further. He had lost his focus at work and consequently his job in a misguided effort to get his wife back, but that never happened. At the time, I was telling the truth when I told him I got no more than a vague feeling, like a conscience, from Revati. He must believe that I am somehow responsible for Revati's non-existence. So thanks to me, he no longer had any of the things he has been working towards for centuries: his wife, his job, and his life Upstairs. And if she was gone for good, then I could be gone from his life too, written off completely.

But the irony was that she did still exist. I just couldn't tell him, lest I find myself the eternal middleman of their love story. I supposed I should be glad he wasn't yelling at me or trying to attack me, but honestly, ignoring me hurt me worse than either of those things.

As I pondered these thoughts, I danced myself closer to where Pete, Hych, Bleid, Ram, and Echidna sat at the tables. Hych had his arm around Echidna's waist, rooting her in place. He seemed to be her keeper. Ram had his arms crossed and a scowl on his face, just like he did the night of Paul and Stewie's Valentine's day party. I thought about that night, deliberately avoiding thinking about the room upstairs where Ram and I shared the best kiss of my entire life.

Nope, nope, don't think about that.

I wondered whatever happened to Gustov, the cute but babbling Viking I had met and assumed was really into cosplay. I now realized that he probably wasn't cosplaying at all. Gods, he was probably an actual Viking from Valhalla! Did he and Lucy hook up after I introduced them? She had been so tight-lipped about it, and then... she thought I died. Tears pricked my eyes, and I turned my face so none of the cartel members would notice until I put a smile back on my face.

I looked at Devil and he smiled at me, then played a very sexy song and used some kind of fog gun to spray the air, much to the crowd's amusement. I got back to dancing, determined to appreciate the lack of Revati's commentary and shut down any kind of self-pity.

I hadn't died, and I had the chance to take out the leaders that allowed Zach to abduct me in the first place. I wondered what Zach's role was with these people. Did he hang out here too, dancing with them? Was he friends with any of them? Or was he just a casual buyer? For some reason, my thinking hadn't gotten that far. I blamed Revati for my inability to think. I decided I'd ask Devil later tonight, after his set. Perhaps I could solve the mystery of the Veruni all on my own.

For now, I needed to focus on the original mission. I needed to get close enough to Echidna to get some DNA. As I danced, I slowed my movements, arched my back, and ran my hands over my body the way the stripper taught me. I glanced at the cartel members again. Each had a sort of lusty, hazed-over look on their face as they watched my dance moves. Echidna & Ram were the exceptions. She looked expectant—as if she were waiting for me to determine my plan of attack, and he seemed to be trying to look anywhere but at me.

I danced closer to the group. Hych's arm had come down, and he was turned a bit away from Echidna as he said something to Ram. I glanced up at Devil. He understood my intentions. It was one of the many potential plans of attack we had gone over, and he kept the music perfect and blew more fog around, putting us in a haze. I was now within just a few feet of the members, their eyes still glued to me.

Almost there.

I danced right up to Echidna's seat and practiced some of my lap dance moves. Hych stood back just a little to watch me. Just enough to give me an in.

Ready, and…

eight

. . .

IN A FLASH, I glued myself to the front of Echidna and kissed her passionately while wrapping my hands in her hair. She didn't seem surprised at all, as if she knew exactly what I had been thinking. At this point, I was pretty certain one of her gifts was mind-reading.

She opened her mouth to me. Her mouth was soft and warm. Her tongue seemed to be forked, and her saliva had a crazy tang to it. It was both terrifying and exhilarating, and it probably lasted about 2 seconds before Hych snapped back into his right senses. He hit the button for whatever the shocker thing was on Echidna's ankle and a shock slammed through her and into me, nearly burning my mouth in the process.

The force of it threw me backward, but I managed to hold on to her hair enough that the force ripped a few pieces out. I lay senseless on the floor for a split second, my eyes closed. When I opened them, I sat up in time to see Hych hurrying off with Echidna in his arms. There were a few of them, and colors in the corners of my vision. In our plan, we hadn't realized that Echidna's saliva would also be a drug. I was WASTED. I stumbled to my feet. Someone was helping me up, but I couldn't be sure who. I realized I was laughing maniacally.

Focus, Focus... the kit. You need the kit!

It took all the concentration in the world, but I stumbled to the bathroom, fortunately located nearby. I was trying hard not to swallow, and my mouth was watering terribly from Echidna's kiss.

I stumbled into the unisex bathroom and locked the door behind me. I clawed at the zipper on my bag while my vision swam. After more struggles, I removed and opened the DNA collection kit. I grabbed the cotton swab, shoved it in my mouth, nearly gagged on it, then stuck it in the ziplock bag with the hairs that were still miraculously wound around my shaky fingers, placing them back inside the plastic, which I jammed inside the metal container of mints in my fanny pack.

I forced myself to vomit to get as much of the drug out of my system as possible, and I rinsed my mouth out with water as best I could, splashing some on my face for good measure before reopening my bag and popping in one of those mints. They were very strong and peppermint flavored. The initial disorienting wave of whatever was in Echidna's saliva seemed to wear off, and my vision was slowly coming back into focus, but I was still quite high.

I stared at myself in the mirror. Trying to get my shit together in bathrooms was becoming an unwelcome new activity.

Deliver the kit!

My inner monologue seemed to echo around in the space in my head Revati had left. The sounds seemed to echo and bounce off the walls and ceiling as well, and then they started warping again. I was nearly done. I could do this, fight this—I just had to get to the drop-off point first. I opened the bathroom door.

"Sugar!" Devil was walking towards me, and he looked worried.

I stumbled backward a bit but caught myself and gave him a smile and a thumbs-up.

"AIR! GOING FOR AIR!" I yelled, dramatically pointing towards the exit.

He knew what that meant: I had succeeded in my mission and now it was just a matter of placing the kit outside in one of the many designated spots for the High Order to retrieve.

He stood halfway between me and his DJ equipment and looked like he was trying to decide what he should do.

"I'M OK, I'LL BE RIGHT BACK!"

He didn't look convinced, but he blew me a kiss and went back to his station. It looked like a few cartel members remained at the booth, but I wasn't sure how many, as my vision was still pretty trippy and the room seemed to pound in on me. I was still wobbly, but I was slightly steadier on my feet as I walked out the club exit into the lobby and through the front doors.

The warm, dry air outside washed over me. I tried to take deep breaths, as if they would heal me somehow, but all they did was make me cough. It was as if I could taste all the despair, loss, heartbreak, and debauchery in the entire city. I was desperate for the moist air so full of life I had known back in the woods in Pennsylvania. With all my inhibitions lowered like this, it took everything I had not to fall apart in a sea of tears right here on the sidewalk.

You're almost done! Keep it together!

I made a sharp left turn and walked up the sidewalk as fast as I could go in the crowd. I crossed the street at a crosswalk another block up. The combination of the lights, the air, the massive screens, the cars, and the crowds felt incredibly oppressive. Someone bumped me, and I had a flash of a woman yelling. Someone else touched me, and a child sobbed behind my eyes. Echidna's saliva was having some serious consequences.

I thought back to the couple at Armagodden. It must've been Echidna's blood Star had wanted to share. Her boyfriend had said that taking it while hurting was not a good idea, and I think I understood now what he was talking about. It was quite alarming, so I tried my best to stay away from the crowd and not touch anyone else—their pain was becoming my own in that touch.

When I reached a wider part of the sidewalk, I gripped one of the short cement poles designed to prevent cars from driving up over the curb as I tried to get my bearings. There were several drop-off points along here, but with my head so full, it was all blending together.

"'Scuse me miss, are you ok?" a deep southern accent asked from behind me.

I opened my eyes and turned around. It took me a minute to process that I was looking at Agent Webber. He was wearing the same sunglasses as before, but he had a different button-down shirt on. This one was slightly baggy, and despite his size, he seemed to fit right into the crowd. Well, he would have, but he seemed to glow a deep, vivid crimson color. I was awestruck.

"You're—uh," I wanted to tell him he was glowing, and then I looked down at my own hands. I was shimmering myself, but I was golden, with teeny-tiny little specks of that same red color swirling and circulating under my skin. I slowly turned my hands to examine them.

"Miss? You having a problem?" He spoke again.

His voice had a completely different cadence and slight southern twang. It was very confusing until my I realized he was probably disguising his voice and pretending to be a stranger, just in case any cartel spies were nearby.

"I'm… just a little lost, I guess."

I wanted to aim for lighthearted, but it was such an

accurate statement in so many ways that my voice broke a little, and my momentary moment of awe flipped back to one of despair.

"Where you trying to get to?"

"Club Omnia, in Caesar's Palace. My husband's there. I just wanted some air," I said, hoping he understood what I was telling him.

I was trying very hard to annunciate the words slowly, clearly, and correctly, so he would get the underlying message: *I've got it, but I lost the drop-off points* but I suspected it only made me sound as wasted as I was.

"Your husband let you out here alone like this?" I couldn't tell if Agent Webber was pretending to be agitated, or if he was truly annoyed that I was out here alone.

I shrugged. "S'ok, I'm ok," I said, and I straightened up from the pole. "but this air is so *sad*, and the people, gods, the *people*..." I leaned towards him. "Don't tell my husband, but... I think I hate it here."

I was aiming for a joking tone again, but I have no idea how I sounded. I leaned back again and put my hand over my eyes. His glowing was making me forget what I was doing, and I still needed to figure this out.

"Fuckfuckfuckfuckfuck," I mumbled."Wait! I know! Can you help?"

It was a struggle, but I managed to unclip my little bag from my waist and unzip it.

"We can have mints! We need mints! *Please*, sir," I jammed my hand into the bag, pulling out the little metal tin that contained both the mints and the little baggie with the swab and the hairs.

I stuck it in his hand, careful not to touch him. I felt such relief that I lowered my other hand and accidentally spilled everything from my bag onto the ground. I got down on all fours to collect my belongings, but my lip stain kept rolling away from me. I tried to crawl after it into the street, but

Agent Webber was there, snatching them up and pulling me back away from the road.

A vision swallowed me up.

Nothingness.

It felt like something should have been there, but it wasn't any longer. The most desperate feeling of loss and despair swamped me, and I cried out.

I opened my eyes, and Webber was now a few feet back from me. He was holding out his hand. He wanted to help me up. I shook my head.

"Nooo, no, please, don't touch me, I'm ok, I just need the Omnia," I wiped my face and felt tears on my cheeks, unsure of when they got there. I stood up, gripping the poll again, and got my bag clipped back on. I looked around, hoping a crowd hadn't gathered. It hadn't. No one seemed to notice. I was just another wasted girl on the strip. I took a breath, and it seemed a little easier. The drug was wearing off.

Agent Webber seemed to glow much less, and I only held a tiny shimmer.

"Can I have my mints back now?" I asked with a tiny smile.

He opened the tin and placed it in my open palm. There was now nothing but mints inside, and I smiled, taking one.

"Do you want one?"

"No, thank you. Stay right here, ok? Can you do that for me, sweetheart?"

He stayed in character, sounding just like a chivalrous and slightly patronizing southern gentleman, or maybe an off-duty police officer.

"You sound like a cop, *sweetheart,*" I laughed at him. "You look like one too. What's with the sunglasses at night?"

I teased him, enjoying the sharp burst of peppermint in

my mouth. It helped counteract all that awfulness the air held before.

"I'll be right back. Don't go anywhere, ok?"

I laughed. The second he left, I started to walk again. I needed to get back to the club now that Agent Webber had the DNA, and I didn't want to risk being seen with him further.

"Hey, hey, that's the wrong way!" He was back again.

I looked up at him. Two beautiful angels with feathered wings flanked him. Ok, they probably weren't actual angels, but they were both smiling and friendly and happily accepting money from him.

"Come on, we're going to get you back to your husband."

Each grabbed one of my arms. Alarmed, I braced for impact, but thankfully no more visions happened. They guided me to the front entrance of Caesar's Palace, not stopping until I was back inside the lobby, the entrance to the club very clear.

By the time I made it back to the DJ booth, I was so exhausted I could barely function, but at least I wasn't tripping out anymore. Devil seemed very relieved to see me.

"You were gone so long, I was worried," He said while hugging me after ending his set.

"I got lost, but a demon in sunglasses paid some feathered angels to get me back," I tried to explain.

"Welcome to Vegas, Sugar," he laughed. "See why I love it here?"

———

The next morning, I was insanely hungover. I don't know if it was just iboga withdrawal or something in Echidna's kiss, but I felt like hell and was hardly rested at all.

For the first time in months, my nightmares about Ram,

which had turned out to be repressed memories of him dying when I was a small child, were back, mixed now with the nothingness and despair I had felt on the sidewalk.

I woke with a heavy sense of loss, picturing Ram's beautiful face staring after me as Devil carried me down the hall after his set the night before. He looked... heartbroken. But that couldn't be, could it? He was the one who left ME. He was the one ignoring ME.

Revati was still crying, though less animated than yesterday. I don't even think she particularly cared that we sent her to the Shadowlands yesterday. It was probably better for her than to have to watch Ram interact with the cartel while ignoring me.

Without thinking, I pulled my necklace out and stroked his ring. I tried not to think about the pain he was causing, but it was impossible to hide it. Revati's crying took on a bitter, angry tone. I felt as if I was nearly drowning in grief and pain, my head just barely above the surface.

Devil came back into the room, a cup of tea in his hand for me. He had gone down to the lobby to fetch it. He set it on the side table and crawled back into bed, snuggling up next to me. He gently took my hands away from my necklace and tucked it back in my sleeping shirt, and wrapped me in his arms.

"You're going to be ok, Sugar. You were amazing last night, you know? You did it! We are almost free of this place forever. Just one more day here. One more day. One more piece of evidence. Afterward, we'll take you wherever you want to go. We'll separate you and Revati, and we'll help heal your heart. We'll give you the best life."

He showered my face with sweet little kisses as he spoke. One more day. I could do this. Revati pepped up at the mention of getting out of my head and into her own body.

It was Sunday, and this morning's requirement was

brunch with the cartel. After carefully sipping my tea, I showered and got dressed. I wore a pair of nice jeans and a silk camisole with spaghetti straps. It was dressier than my preferred comfort clothes, but still much more casual than the sexy club clothes I rocked last night. I would have to don something similar for Introspection's final set tonight, but I was feeling like I needed more coverage as armor to go into this brunch.

As we approached the gang at the restaurant, I had no idea what to expect as a greeting. I hadn't seen any of them since they had shocked me as I made out with Echidna and fell to the floor, laughing insensibly.

Apparently, the whole affair was going to be politely ignored. I guess it's true what they say about Vegas. Unfortunately, the seating arrangement was the same as last night. I took a seat next to Ram and wished everyone a good morning.

"His hair! AAAAAhhhhhhh!!!" Revati wailed.

I winced. She had been in the Shadowlands during last night's dinner, and like me, had been so shocked at his appearance the first time that she hadn't taken in the details. This was the first she saw his haircut. For reasons I couldn't delve into now, lest I seem entirely insane, I couldn't ask her why it caused a fresh wave of such deep, deep despair. Ram stared down at his tea as if my presence meant nothing. Pete smirked, looking back and forth between Ram, Devil, and myself before he spoke.

"Quite the show last night, Naoma! Or should I say Chuli?"

I looked up sharply, studying him. Devil looked alarmed and angry. Although I was posing as myself, Pete shouldn't have known about my former name unless he was doing some serious digging. There wasn't anything further for him to find, but his keen interest in me was still concerning.

"I don't know why it took me so long to put it together! Amazing." he laughed. "Intro, mate, truly a man of your word!" and he took a minute to eat a bite of a muffin from the plate in front of him.

I was getting a very uneasy feeling as Devil and I locked eyes. His look could only be described as apologetic. The rest of the table stared at Pete, waiting for him to finish. He looked at them all as he swallowed, then gestured to me.

"This is the girl. The princess."

His meaning still didn't seem to register with anyone. He rolled his eyes.

"Zach's Princess? Come on, you guys were all here for that!"

Now they were all staring back and forth between me and Devil. My heart began pounding in fear. Whatever was happening, I suspected it wasn't good, wasn't good at all. I wanted to scream at Pete to shut up. I knew he was about to say something devastating. I could tell by the gleam in his eye.

"If you all recall, Zach was here, waxing poetic about his long-lost princess, and how he was going to make her his. He claimed he didn't need the Veruni, of course, but felt it would be handy to have, just in case."

"Shut up, Pete," Devil lashed out angrily, rising out of his seat a bit. He was pushed back down by Hych's brawny arm on his shoulder.

"She doesn't even know, does she?" He sounded amazed and laughed again. Now he turned to me.

"Let me enlighten you, you sweet little naïve thing."

He smirked in that irritating way of a man who thinks he's smarter than a woman.

"Intro here got into it with Zach after he agreed to sell him the Veruni. He told him he was such a loser that he knew he'd fail, even with drugs. He then told him…"

I felt the color drain from my face.

"What!?" Revati gasped.

Devil was the one who had given Zach the Veruni.

Pete continued.

"Intro told him that when he failed, he would track down his princess, convince her to marry him, and then, and I quote here, 'fuck her senseless until it's my name she screams,' end quote. Zach was so mad! Ha! But judging from the sounds I heard from your room yesterday, I would say you've really kept your word, mate. Bravo!"

He laughed and clapped his hands as my entire world fell apart. Again.

I looked at Devil with fresh eyes, like a veil had been lifted.

I was wrong to trust him.

Horrified and enraged, Revati shouted an epitaph of curse words at him. It was shocking to hear her curse, and also satisfying, since I needed to remain silent for a moment while I figured out how to get out of this situation safely.

Pete obviously thrived on chaos and destruction, and I didn't want to give him any indication he was destroying me from the inside out. I calmly took a sip of my tea, then shrugged my shoulder, as if none of this was news to me.

"You knew this?" Pete looked confused.

"What kind of fool would I have to be not to know?"

"But—"

"But what? Introspection is smarter and more clever than Zach ever was."

I looked at Devil poignantly, and I hoped the betrayal and hatred I felt for him at that moment came across as a heated desire to the rest of the table.

"And," Pete was determined not to lose his bravado, "THIS blockhead!" He now gestured to Ram. "What kind of idiot Old God do you have to be to get captured and TORTURED by that Forgotten little son of a bitch, and then get rescued by a Lost? No wonder you got fired! The shame you must feel when you think about it. No wonder you avoid looking at her!" and he laughed long and hard.

I didn't dare look at Ram. I could only imagine the feelings those comments must've dredged up. Bleid piped up, cutting off Pete's laughter.

"Did you really plunge a dagger in Zach's neck?"

I nodded, fighting off all the horrendous feelings thinking about that moment caused in me.

"How very barbarian. I approve." He smiled.

It was very chilling. I stood up on my shaky legs.

"Excuse me, everyone, I find that I'm not as hungry as I had thought." I stood up from the table.

A fit of inspiration took me, and I walked over to Pete and picked up his napkin, and then leaned over the table in a way that gave him a flash of my cleavage while I placed his half-eaten muffin on top in my hand.

"This looks good for later though. Thanks for splitting it with me," I said, winking. Then I saucily walked out of the place.

I made it back to the room, but I felt numb.

"What do we do now?!" Revati was panicking.

Even though there was no one around and I could easily talk to her, I couldn't find any words at all to say, either out loud or in my head. It was too much.

I put the napkin and the muffin inside a paper bag. I took a swig from the whiskey bottle still sitting there from yesterday, a day that felt light-years away in the past. Still numb, I walked out to the nearest exit and found one of the drop-off points, a much easier thing to accomplish in the daytime while not tripping, and put the bag there.

The sun was blasting everything with its light and heat. The heat felt like it was scorching both my insides and my outsides. Technically, I supposed I was done with the mission since I now had gathered all evidence needed.

"I tried to tell you not to trust him!" Revati yelled.

Shut up!

I yelled at her, but the anger was all fueled towards myself and she knew it. I really shouldn't have trusted him.

"Just leave, Girl. Walk away right now. Call Agent Webber. He will get you home," Revati told me.

Perhaps it would have worked better if I actually had a home. *What home, Revati!? What home?*

She sighed, probably realizing I was right. We didn't have a home, and neither of us wanted to go back to aimlessly wandering the streets of New York.

We just have to face this. We'll figure out the rest.

"Will they still help us separate, you think? Angel will at least, yes?" Revati asked.

It won't hurt to ask, but...

I didn't have to explain to her the feelings of mistrust, desperation, and the one small thread of hope just barely hanging on. I was sure she felt them throughout my whole body.

nine

. . .

I GOT BACK in as the golden rays of the late afternoon sun beamed through the partially opened curtains. Devil was sitting in an upholstered chair in the corner. When he saw me, he stood up and began walking towards me. I shrunk back, away from him.

"Sugar, please.."

But he stopped walking, stretching out his arm towards me.

"Don't touch me."

At my proclamation, his hand went limp and returned to his side as he sighed.

"I should've known that sneaky bastard would tell you."

"You should have known!? I—" I was so upset and angry that I was nearly choking on my own words, "—I should have been the one to fucking know!!"

"Sugar, shhhh… please keep your voice down. It's not safe here."

Unfortunately, my logical and self-preserving side knew he was right. I wanted to scream in his face and slap him, but I also wanted to live long enough to get out of this godforsaken—more like god-swarmed—hotel in this hellhole of a city. I closed my eyes and practiced box breathing, a technique that was supposed to help with anxiety.

Inhale, count to 4. Exhale, and count to 4. Inhale, count to 4. Exhale, and count to 4. Inhale, count to 4. Exhale, and count to 4.

I tried to imagine myself back in the woods of Bear Mountain: my former refuge. This act gave me just enough peace to keep my rage and hurt from spiraling out of control. I opened my eyes again before I descended into despairing homesickness. It was time to start asking questions.

"Did Angel know?"

"He knew about the marriage bet, just not the… details."

I thought about Pete joking about my screams from yesterday and nearly gagged.

"He wanted me to tell you, but I made him promise to wait until after the mission. I didn't think you'd do it if you knew, and you really are perfect for this."

I scoffed. He was probably right about one thing, at least. I don't think I could have ever said yes, knowing what I know now.

Pretending at the brunch table for a moment this morning was hard enough, and getting through tonight was going to be even harder. Each time I thought of the bet, and that he was ultimately responsible for giving Zach the Veruni, the knowledge tore my heart apart a little further.

"He doesn't know about the Veruni either," I stated.

Angel would have never allowed that to happen. Devil nodded solemnly.

"It's one of the only things I've ever hidden from him. A fan gave it to me at a show in Belgium—his name was Tom. Or maybe Toby? I don't know how he got it. I found it fascinating, but I didn't plan to use it or sell it. Zach was there when I told the cartel about it. He was such an annoying little twat, it seemed like a fun challenge. I didn't think through what the human consequences would be." He had the good graces to look ashamed.

"I gave the lead to the High Order, but I couldn't tell Angel. He would have been so disappointed in me, and I hate disappointing him. I hate disappointing you just as much." He looked as if that admission surprised him. "If I knew you then, if I could take it back…"

I scoffed again. I was feeling a whole lot of feelings right now: rage, hurt, and mistrust. Disappointed didn't even begin to cover it.

I had killed someone and watched the life seep out of him. Even if he deserved it, it was something I never wanted to see ever again. An innocent woman had died in an explosion at my house. People's lives had been ruined. My life had been incinerated. He could have prevented all of it from happening. I paced the room.

"Let's go! Please, let's just leave! We'll go back to Angel. We need to get out of here! Start packing!!" Revati barked at me.

As much as I wanted to agree with her for once, I didn't want to let any of these stupid gods believe they scared off this pathetic little Lost girl. I wanted to stick around and watch when the High Order busted in and took them all away.

I wasn't sure how long it took to identify god and creature DNA, but we had gone over a scenario where if they received everything they needed, they might be able to bust them within hours.

I wanted those bastards to know it was ME that destroyed their business.

I had a quick and painful flash of Ram getting caught up in it. Part of me wanted to warn him, but he made his own choices. He knew the risks.

Revati was still clinging to the idea that there was some

kind of misunderstanding and she pleaded for me to tell him. But if I tipped him off, how could I know he wouldn't just tip the cartel off? He couldn't be bothered enough to acknowledge my existence, so why should I care about his future? And besides, there was a gag order on the whole mission. I was through risking my life for him.

I pushed all these hurts away for the moment and I pulled my shit together—again—and formulated a plan. I looked at the clock. It was a little after 4:00. I had a hot stone massage booked at the spa at 5:30, my favorite. If I left now, I had time to take advantage of the roman baths, steam room, and hydro showers first. I was a sucker for a good spa, and it might give me the vitality needed to get through this one last night. Physically, I was still feeling pretty terrible thanks to my hangover, high-heeled dancing, and electrocution combo from last night, not to mention the emotional gut punch this morning.

Before I left, I knew I needed to give Devil some kind of response.

"I'll be on the dance floor tonight."

Devil nodded, and he seemed slightly relieved, and then I continued.

"Once these fuckers are rounded up, you and Angel will help me and Revati. After that, I'm filing for divorce. It makes me sick to look at you now. I never want to see you again."

I turned away from the hurt look on his face, stuck my key card in my pocket, and headed down the hall towards the spa, barefoot. I was feeling pretty weak, and I realized I hadn't eaten anything since those few precious bites of soup the night before. I decided I'd call room service when I got back from my massage. Maybe they still had that soup.

ten

. . .

ram

AS I SAT at the brunch table, I watched Chuli—no, Naoma —walk away from me for the fourth time in the past 24 hours, each time taking another piece of my heart with her, helpless to do anything about it.

I tried to stay calm and collected and mostly succeeded. I'd nearly crushed my own hand under the table with the desire to destroy each and every person at this horrendous gathering, especially Pete and Introspection, but a clear mind was essential for what was to come. I couldn't afford to allow my emotions to cloud my judgment this time around, especially when I was so close to learning everything I needed to know to put this crew out of Earth business.

It wouldn't do to kill only some of them. They were like the Hydra. I had to make sure I knew where every head was located before I struck. Even if every member came straight back downstairs to Earth, it would take them decades to recover, if not longer.

I'd deliberately begun my plan focused only on the parts that involved selling a small amount of Soma for cash, which was true enough. I didn't feel too terrible selling it, since down here on Earth, it was basically the equivalent of Ritalin. It helped the drinker stay focused and alert; nothing that could be deemed very harmful.

It had belonged to Yamuna, the river goddess I'd offended all those years ago, and the money would go to her. I finally reconnected with her and apologized for my actions all those years ago, when I was what Naoma had called "a pompous douche" after being drugged with Veruni. She ran an environmental charity to help keep her waters clean from the constant threats of pollution, and my generous donation probably helped pave the way for her forgiveness. I cemented it when I got my famous brother and sister-in-law to bring attention to her charity and the state of the river.

I deliberately hadn't worked out the next part of the plan, or Introspection would have seen right through me, just like that last time. It was a few years ago, back when I was a brand new agent. The High Order had hoped my complete lack of history with them would benefit me, since I had no traceable record as an agent. I didn't know what it was that Introspection saw when he shook my hand, but he had just laughed and told me good luck with the High Order, and they had escorted me outside.

This time around, I hoped my general outrage and anger at the High Order would work in my favor, so long as I didn't allow myself to dwell on the fact that my anger had everything to do with how little they were doing to put this cartel out of business, and nothing to do with my getting fired. After I had failed so spectacularly, I didn't blame them one bit for turning me out.

Now that I had passed Introspection's test, I had access

to the entire cartel. I would hang around with these degenerates as long as needed to determine how best to take them out, since the High Order seemed so content with letting them continue to spread their malicious wares on Earth.

The rest of my punishment had seemed difficult, but doable. After all, I was the same God who spent many yugas carrying a load of guilt and uncertainty on my shoulders. My followers still turned to me to pray for the strength to get through difficult situations. What were a few more months of uncertainty? They had gone by tolerably enough in the beginning. Painful? Absolutely. But tolerable, until I set foot in Pete's office yesterday.

Since then, each moment I saw her, it felt like time slowed down, and I was slowly crawling through a nightmare. I still hadn't figured out the role of that strange woman with the golden eyes, either, and if she was a friend or foe. Each time she stared at me, I got chills. Something about her seemed familiar. Once, I got the impression that she was about to communicate with my mind in the same way that animals do, but then she turned away, and I hadn't felt anything like it since.

She appeared to have some kind of intoxicating effect on Naoma. Had she known that was going to happen when she kissed her? And why did they both fall to the floor? It took every ounce of control I had not to check on her when that happened.

I brought myself back to the present moment. The table seemed to shrug off Naoma's exit, Introspection included, though I swore I saw a flash of apology and pain on his face when Pete first brought up Zach. She played it off beautifully, but there was no way she knew Introspection's involvement, right? Nothing about her marriage to Introspection — a thought that felt like a knife slicing into the scar on my chest each time I thought it—made sense.

Apparently, the High Order left her in the dark about what happened to me. It was infuriating. It ripped me apart further to wonder what she must think of me now that I was ignoring her. Was it any wonder she was lashing out, getting wasted, and making out with strangers? Acting wild was one thing, but why did she have to get married? And to the very man that had sold Zach the Veruni at that?

No, she couldn't have known that. She had to have an excellent reason, but it mystified me what it could be.

But now what? Even if she hadn't known Introspection was the Veruni source until now, she had cared about him enough to marry the bastard. Even if she now hated him, I couldn't just kill her husband, right? She'd hate me even more than she already did. There was no disguising the disgust in her voice when she accused me of being in league with the cartel. But why was she also here, if she was so disgusted by them? Did she not realize they were a cartel until today? What had Introspection told her?

After all that we had been through, I was back to being seen as a grumpy and untrustworthy asshole. Just like before, there was so much I wanted, no—NEEDED to tell her, but couldn't. I broke the promise I made to myself to tell her the truth from now on, no matter what, back when she had nearly died of frostbite. I hadn't realized I'd be forced to make an exception to that promise.

I was deeply worried about her. I'd been too late to save my wife all those years ago, but I worked hard these past few months to put my past to rest. I had officially given up on rescuing Revati and finally accepted the fact that she was not coming back. I'd shaved my head just after leaving Pennsylvania, a symbolic beginning to a formal grieving process.

I couldn't bear the thought of losing Naoma too. The path she was on seemed reckless and self-destructive. Even if she didn't choose me, she deserved happiness, security, and safety, not this fucked up, dangerous cartel world.

Just one more day.

Tomorrow, before she left, I would find a way to talk to her alone, Introspection be damned, cartel be damned. No —I wouldn't even wait until the morning. I would find her at the stroke of midnight, and she could finally hear the truth about everything, including my feelings for her, now that I had time to sort them out.

———

They requested me at dinner at 5:00 this evening. Pete was to complete negotiations with me over the price and logistics of the Soma. After that, I was free to leave, but I wouldn't leave until I had that heart-to-heart with Naoma.

I had been thinking about her all day, and dreaming of seeing her again. So basically, today was just like any other day. I remembered the first time I saw her and my embarrassing reaction. I had fainted, of all things. Tonight was going to be the exact opposite. I was going in prepared.

I got to the restaurant a few minutes early and was sitting at the bar, nursing a seltzer on ice with a lime. It was Naoma who taught me this trick, way back at the Valentine's Party. That night, she also taught me that my mouth was made for kissing her, but I couldn't dare think about that now. Drinking a fake cocktail helped me to blend in with drinkers, to not call attention to myself. It was a handy trick indeed, and often got people to open up more.

I had been doing this with Bleid for some time now. The wolfish prick was how I found my way inside the cartel this time around. He had confided, after a few alcoholic drinks, that he usually felt a bit like an outsider himself, and he was very happy to have someone he could gossip with. I just nodded and smiled at the right times, and he told me more about each of the cartel members, far more than any of them would have ever said themselves. I didn't even think he realized just how much intel had slipped from his drunken lips.

Over the last two months, I learned about their weaknesses, the things they cared about, where they did the bad things, and what they did with themselves when they weren't here. All things that would help me pick them off.

The more time I spent hearing Bleid spew his vile thoughts, especially his views on women, the more I looked forward to his demise. It was frustrating how long it had taken to get on the agenda of the official monthly Vegas meeting. I was hoping to have the cartel entirely wiped out by now, but Bleid insinuated that something big was happening these last few months, and I needed to wait my turn.

After replaying the facts all afternoon in between my thoughts of Naoma, I suspected the big-ticket item Bleid was referring to was the golden-eyed woman. She might not be a woman at all, but a dangerous creature, especially after her kiss left Naoma so wasted. Once again, I tried not to think too hard about the kissing part. I knew all too well what Naoma's kisses felt and tasted like, and it just about killed me to watch her handing them out like candy.

Naoma and the woman, whose name I still didn't know, had both dropped as if they were shocked somehow. The woman's powers might have involved some kind of shocking pain, but it seemed more likely they were both somehow zapped by something else. I now felt certain the golden-eyed woman was being held captive. I hoped to get a better look at her later this evening, so I knew how best to proceed. I would also try to communicate with her with my power.

Of the cartel, Introspection was the most mysterious. He was an Old God, but no one seemed to know who he was or how he knew the things he knew, but they all seemed content enough to know he was a sort-of a psychic body-guard against the High Order. I wasn't the only one surprised to discover he had married, though I was prob-ably the only one completely gutted by that knowledge. I was determined to learn more about Introspection, not only because of his role in the cartel, but to help protect Naoma, and to help free her, if that's what she desired.

Bleid came up and got a beer and sat next to me. He had a disturbing gleam in his eye, as if he had something juicy he wanted to say. But everyone else was arriving as well, so we left the bar and took our seats at the table.

Introspection arrived without Naoma and took up his usual spot. Hydd and the golden-eyed woman were also missing. Pete smirked at Introspection and gestured to the empty seat next to me.

"Where's your lovely wife this evening? Trouble in paradise, mate?"

Introspection laughed. "What, you thought you'd dropped some kind of intel at brunch, Pete, and stirred up trouble?"

He rolled his eyes at Pete's attempt. Pete looked annoyed. That was exactly what he had been doing.

"Honestly. Such childishness. She is at the spa. My wife deserves to be pampered, not to be subjected to intruding asshats like you." he smiled after he said it, as if it were playful banter.

"We know where she is," said Mr. Godwin solemnly. "Where did you meet her?"

Introspection gave him a surprised glance, but spoke. "The first time I saw her, she was on the street on a sunny morning in New York City. The sun was on her head. I caught her reflection in a window. Her eyes spoke volumes.

I was smitten. She is beautiful, no? I followed her home. When I saw her with Paul from Burning Wind, I realized she was Zach's *objet petit a*."

Everyone kind of gave little nods of appreciation or understanding. In the god crowd, Paul was a bit of a celebrity, like a life coach. Everyone had at least heard of his publishing press, and his ability to help Forgettens regain some power by gaining new earthly followers.

"I saw her again at Armagodden. She had snuck into the VIP lounge. Instead of fearing my power, she welcomed it. She took my hand and let me in. Inside, she has such beauty, such sweetness, such bravery! But she was also so alone, so scared to trust." he made a pointed glance in my direction. "And then, she danced. I was more than smitten this time, boys—I was in love."

He closed his eyes for a moment and smiled as if he was enchanted all over again. Everyone at the table had seen her dancing the night before, a sight I deliberately turned away from before I forgot all the reasons I was there. She had always been powerful on the dance floor, but now, she was positively enchanting.

"I knew she must be mine. The bet was a happy accident. Making her happy is something worth living for." He smiled again, the smile of a man truly and well-smitten.

I thought he saw a trace of sadness there for a moment, but it vanished before I could be sure.

"So I dared her to marry me. And she did."

"Mmmm. But why is she...here?"

Mr. Godwin inquired again.

"We share everything. We have no secrets. Where I go, she goes. I am not afraid to show her my talents, or my friends." With this he gestured around to the people at the table, deliberately lowering his hand and eyes before he included me in the gesture.

It was very clear what he thought of me.

sara ruch

"And you trust her entirely?" Pete chimed in.

"With my life," Introspection replied in a very matter-of-fact way.

"And you've known her for how long, oh besotted one?"

Introspection appeared to be doing the math in his head. "It has been...about 12 days since I first saw her."

"And you married her. And you brought her here. To meet us."

"Of course! I would not leave her so soon after marrying her! She doesn't care what you do. She likes to party. You saw yourself. Was that kiss with your new lady friend hot or what! That was like an explosion. You should have seen her in the strip club, seducing the dancers. I suspect I have many exciting bedroom adventures ahead of me this Earth spin, boys. How lucky I am," and he laughed again, as if he had won some kind of sexy wife lottery.

Unfortunately for me, it appeared that he had.

"What was your wedding like?" Pete asked.

The level of questioning seemed to get more intense. Bleid glanced at me again with that same gleam. I got a very uneasy feeling. No one ever asked so many questions about fellow cartel members' personal lives, as far as I knew.

Something was wrong. I was sure Introspection could feel it, too. He had to, right? But he went right on as if he had nothing to worry about. Perhaps he didn't. Perhaps they were just curious about the love life of their most mysterious member.

"It was so American and silly! Elvis married us in rented clothing. We gave Elvis lyric vows. We danced back down the aisle."

He laughed, and it reached his eyes as he took a sip of coffee. He was very happy recalling his wedding day. I felt another pang of jealousy, but I swallowed it down.

"Yes, those dance moves looked practically rehearsed," Pete chimed in, smiling slightly.

Introspection carefully set his coffee cup down and lifted his napkin to his lips.

"Surely you wouldn't think a wedding that charming wouldn't be posted on the chapel's Youtube channel for anyone to find. Pete found it this afternoon and showed it to some of us. It was impressive indeed," Mr. Godwin said.

Introspection's easy smile came back. "You see then? Naoma was born to dance."

"We've been talking about it," Pete replied, "and decided that this spontaneous marriage of yours deserves a special kind of celebration. We've canceled your set tonight, mate. Instead, we'll be taking you out. Think of it as a little... post-bachelor party."

Introspection continued to smile obliviously, but I felt even more uneasy than before. This couldn't be good at all. Bleid was smiling an awful smile, Gil joining in.

"Great," Introspection said, rising from the table. "Let me just go tell Naoma she's on her own tonight, and I'll get changed into something nicer, if it's required?"

"No need. We sent someone around to talk to her," Pete said, smirking.

"Cool," Introspection said, coming around the table.

Everyone else was rising now too, including me. I was trying to pick up on any more tension, to figure out where this was going when Introspection approached me.

"But not this fucker, right? I can't imagine having a good time with his ugly mug glaring at me the whole time. He's always glaring at my wife, despite my warnings."

He got in my face, angry. I could feel Introspection's dark power building. I thought Intro had much bigger problems to worry about at the moment, but I stood my ground and glared right back.

"Leave my wife alone, motherfucker! It's not her fault you're incompetent!" He pushed me, hard.

I was not an easy God to push around, and I didn't budge on the outside. But on the inside, my patience was crumbling. I tried to hold in my emotions, but Intro knew just which buttons to push, so he continued.

"She trusts ME! She loves ME!"

All my jealousy and frustration and anger at what Intro had done to Naoma poured out, and I lost it and punched him. Intro grabbed right back onto me. The two of us were surprisingly well-matched, despite his smaller stature. We each got in a few good blows before they pulled us apart.

"He can stay with me," Bleid said, pulling me towards the exit that led to the casino.

Mr. Godwin gave him a silent nod of approval. The rest of the group went the other direction, towards the back exit, flanking Introspection quite closely. When they were gone, Bleid laughed.

"Oh, do I have a surprise for you! You are going to love this! What justice, what revenge! Ha Ha!" Bleid's laugh was a very ominous sound.

I followed him out, smoothing my clothes back into place as I walked, trying to calm my thoughts. I stopped for a moment to adjust my belt, which had gotten twisted in the fracas, when I felt something sticking out of my pocket. It was a torn and folded piece of napkin. I didn't recall ever putting anything in his pocket, and I opened it.

It was hard to read, as if it had been hastily scribbled by someone who was writing without looking. Three words were haphazardly sprawled across it.

Owl Crow Nest

I discreetly tucked it back in my pocket and caught up

with Bleid as my thoughts spun and then clicked, much like the roulette wheels we were passing by at the moment. I needed a new plan, fast. But first, I needed to see what Bleid wanted to show me. I suspected I already knew what it was, and my heart filled with fear and dread as we followed the signs leading to the spa.

eleven

. . .

Naoma

I sat on my towel and leaned against the wet, hot tiles in the back corner of the steam room. I breathed deep, letting the moisture and the eucalyptus essential oils permeate my lungs and naked skin. It was dark in here, the only light coming through the thick glass door to the room. My headache seemed to lift, and I felt the tension in my muscles start to release.

I was still dreading tonight, but now that I had some time to relax and soak and now steam, I was feeling like I just might be able to seem carefree for a few more hours out there on the dance floor.

Once we were done with this place, I would next focus all my attention on the Shadowlands quest. Honestly, it didn't hurt to focus on something like that now.

Revati, what is it like there?

I interrupted her seemingly endless nostalgic babble about her life Upstairs to ask.

"I was just telling you. We had a room similar to this, and my maidens would use jasmine blossoms and.."

No, not there. There. The Shadowlands.

She got quiet for a moment. "It's dark. There is nothing."

Like nothing, nothing? Did you try to go anywhere?

"No, why would I? I am not going to wander off in the dark all alone. What if I get lost?"

Is there a path or anything?

"I think so. There is a feeling of gravel, and a feeling of soft earth. Perhaps I was on a path, or at least the edge of it."

Did you see anyone else?

"No, it's dark. I told you. I just sit there and wait."

So you never even tried to find anything else out while you were there, knowing that we'll have to go there together one day to get you free?

"Why should I wander? It's bad enough just sitting there. It's... very lonely."

I felt pretty frustrated with her. She could have taken the opportunity to learn more about the place that's going to get us free, and she just... sat there. And then I felt a twinge of guilt. No one should have to feel so alone all the time.

Once we are separated, you won't be lonely. You can have as many maidens and friends and suitors as you'd like. You can talk to them all day and all night.

"I don't want any other suitors. I want my husband!" she said, and cried again.

I felt my headache slip back in, and the tension in my shoulders come back.

Revati, please, for the love of gods, just stop crying, I begged, hanging my head down.

A shadow at the door interrupted our silent conversation. A woman entered, her features silhouetted by the light behind her and the steam cloud. As the door closed behind her, I heard the distinct snick of a deadbolt being locked from the outside.

Shit, shit, shit.

I sat up, on alert. The woman gracefully slithered towards me. As she got closer, her eyes appeared to illuminate from within, with a golden color.

Echidna.

She sat down next to me and turned to face me.

"Fear me not, sister."

She was speaking somehow, but not out loud. It was more of an impression in my mind.

I'm not afraid of you, I replied in my mind, in case someone was listening at the door.

Perhaps I should have been, but so far I'd gotten nothing but the impression that she was—maybe not friendly, but at least open to whatever it was I was trying to accomplish.

"I speak to Revati. She was not here before."

Now here was someone else that knew about Revati. Some secret she was turning out to be!

"You know my name? Who are you?" Revati's voice seemed to hold equal amounts of fear and awe.

"I have many names, sister. This girl knows me as Echidna. You know me as something else."

"Manasa!? Is that you? What are you doing here? I thought you were exiled from Earth!"

Revati's voice grew louder in her excitement. I winced. My head was getting to be a very crowded place, and their conversation was adding extra pressure to my headache. Echidna, aka Manasa, smiled, her eyes crinkling into slits when she did so.

"It's true. I should not be here. Does the High Order know me as Manasa, girl?"

I shook my head. *I can't be sure, but I don't think so.*

It was pretty interesting that the goddess known as the mother of monsters to the Greeks could be the very same one known as the goddess of snakes to Hindus, but she hid that knowledge from other gods. I wondered for a moment how all the various pantheons intersected. A part of me got very excited when I realized I might just be able to find out, straight from the horses' mouths, but then I recalled the sound of the lock, and that I was potentially in a lot of trouble at the moment.

"I thought you were Lost, Revati. If we had time, I would have liked to hear the story of how you are sharing this girl's body sometimes, and why your husband no longer speaks to you, and I would like to tell you both the tale of how I became captured by these vile men, but I fear we have no more time. You, girl, have been discovered as a traitor. I cannot enter the minds of men, but I hear them speak. They intend to capture your husband at dinner, and then someone will return for us. I trust you got what you needed from me yesterday?"

Yes, your DNA went to the High Order. They now have the proof they need to shut down this cartel.

I managed to explain myself, but my heart thumped loudly, and my breathing picked up. How could we have been so stupid? Pete had been working hard, connecting the dots. His brunch conversation made that much clear. I should have known if they dug that far that they had somehow figured out the truth, but his talk about Veruni had blindsided me, and I wasn't thinking clearly. I supposed Devil had been distracted as well.

I wondered how soon the High Order would get here. Would they find me before the cartel came back? What were they going to do with Devil? And why did someone always try to kidnap me naked from a locker room? I thought back to my last kidnapping episode at the gym. Things had seemed hopeless then too, but somehow, I escaped.

I made myself a promise that if I got out of here alive that I was never going to any kind of gym or spa ever again. I stood up and paced back and forth in front of the door, pulling on the handle and then the pins.

"They have locked me in this steam room many times, girl. There is no way out."

What a weird place to put her.

Why do they lock you in the steam room?

"My form is not suited for Earth. I need the steam to survive. There is no way for me to escape from here, just tiles and steam."

Echidna got a strange smile on her face and stalked toward where I was standing, alarming me.

"I am sorry I cannot save you, girl, but perhaps you can save me?"

I'm sorry? How can I save you?

"Kill me."

No! Not again!

I backed away from her. That awful feeling of watching the life drain from Zach came back, and I shuddered.

"It is the only way. Please. You can free me, unlocking the door to the Upstairs. I will simply be reborn up there in my home. How I have suffered here! The things those men made me do! Please, girl. I beg you."

Echidna touched my arm, and a flash of images poured into my brain of her horrible treatment here with the cartel: dark and painful and violent images. It was just like my visions at Armagodden and on the street last night. Kissing her had temporarily transferred some of that power.

I closed my eyes and tried to breathe deeply. I was feeling dizzy and nauseous. It was tricky to get worked up in a steam room. I sat back down and tried to calm myself. I placed my head between my knees.

"Please, help her. It's only right."

Revati shocked the hell out of me with that little request. The woman who didn't even want me to curse or wear pants was over here condoning murder all of a sudden.

How?

I asked. There was no point even considering if there wasn't even a way to do it. Echidna stood in front of me and took my hands in hers.

"Smother me with these."

My hands were shaky. I couldn't do this, could I?

What if the High Order is on its way to free us?

I asked with a hopeful tone.

"Revati is right. I am exiled from Earth. Those Who Judge have decreed it. If I am discovered as Manasa on Earth, they will not care that I was brought here against my will. I will be punished severely. Those Who Judge have no mercy for those that break their rules."

She shuddered and stepped a little farther away from me, as if they were so fearsome she didn't want me to accidentally see her memories. I appreciated that. So it seemed that her options were to be abused by the High Order, or abused by the cartel. Both sounded horrendous.

"They are both horrible. Truly."

I took in one last deep breath through my nose and acquiesced. Echidna lifted her hands and tugged a small ring off her finger. I hadn't noticed it before in the dark, but now I saw it had a jewel embedded, tiny and glittering. She sat down next to me and reached around my neck, unclasping the necklace that held Ram's ring. Despite his betrayal, I was still wearing the damn thing. She slid her ring on the chain next to his and then put the necklace back on me. Revati let out a little sound of reverie.

"A sliver of Nagamani. May it bring you life when you need it most."

Nagamani sounded familiar, but I was too busy preparing for murder to ask any more questions right now. We were out of time. If we talked further, I may chicken out, or someone may come for us.

She kissed the top of my head and then placed herself at

my feet, positioning herself between my legs so I could have a better grip on her. She leaned back and smiled a smile of perfect peace and tranquility.

To an outsider, we probably looked like some kind of silent erotic boudoir photo shoot, our arms and legs entwined, our skin glistening with sweat. We certainly did not look like a murderer and a willing victim. But there was no one there to see us, and no telling when someone would come and if they would be friend or foe, so we needed to do this now.

I tried to force my hands toward her nose and mouth, but I just couldn't seem to make them move. Finally, she used her own hands to gently guide mine into place, then she gently patted them and let go.

Nothing happened for what seemed an eternity, but eventually, her arms and legs thrashed about of their own accord. She was smaller and thinner than I was, so I had no trouble physically overpowering her. I somehow found the resolve to keep my hands restricting her airflow, even though all the good parts of my soul seemed to scream at me to let her live. After two final kicks, she went still. I waited and counted to 60 just to be certain she wasn't just passed out, but she didn't stir.

I dropped my hands to my sides. Echidna's body slipped down my legs. I squatted down and laid her body on the floor. Those golden eyes were still open, but their glowing had faded to black.

She was dead, killed by my own two hands.

I kneeled next to her and closed her eyes. Revati was saying something in another language, or perhaps she was singing, but it seemed like she was coming from underwater. As I watched, Echidna's body dissolved into powdery crystals. It was how I would imagine vampires turned to ash. I couldn't hear anything except the rush of my blood and my ragged breaths.

Breath. Blood. Breath. Blood.

I think I was in shock. I don't know how long I sat there like that, but at some point, sound and life seemed to kick back in.

"Get up! Get up! Someone is coming!!" Revati was desperately yelling at me.

I hopped up and grabbed my damp towel off the seat and twisted it up to use as a whip. I backed up into the corner of the wall that contained the door, anchoring my feet against the slippery floor, crouched myself into some kind of battle stance, and faced the door.

I decided my best chance at escape was to bolt for the door before anyone saw me in the dark steam. I could hear a key being inserted in the door, and someone talking. From the voice, it sounded like Hydd, Echidna's keeper, talking to someone else.

"I mean, I don't know man, you do you, I guess. They didn't specify how to get her to talk. They just told me to hold her here until someone came to get her. Lucky for me, she was already in the steam room. Easiest capture ever. Hands off the snaky piece, though. She gives me the creeps, but you're into some sick shit, man, and you might damage her permanently."

The reply came, but at that point, another burst of steam penetrated the room and obscured the sound and I couldn't hear the voices anymore. From what I had heard so far, that was probably for the best, anyway. Revati cried in terror.

Shut up, shut up!

I willed her, and she tried her best to be quiet. The door opened. Hydd looked around in the darkness and saw the pile of glittery dust formerly known as Echidna's body.

"Oi!" he yelled and stepped forward, clear of the door frame, still holding the door open.

I didn't wait any longer, and I bolted. I slid a bit as I ducked under his arm, but I made it through. There were

two people outside, but I didn't wait long enough to identify them. The first tried to grab for me, but I threw my
towel at his face and kept going. I ran into the next room,
the one with the showers, bathroom stalls, and lockers. I
dove for my locker, ripped it open, and grabbed my bag,
then ran out the door and into the men's locker room across
the way, and dove into one of the many stalls there, hoping
I bought myself a few more minutes before any security
cameras saw me. I threw my jeans and shirt on as fast as I
could, no easy feat with my skin still so wet, but I was
determined to be dressed this time around, and I would
stand out on camera a lot more if I were naked.

I strapped on my bag and stilled myself so I could hear.
There were deep muffled voices coming from the women's
locker room, but the men's room was silent. I crept out of
the stall, listening for any sound, and going over a map of
the building in my head as I headed out the locker room
doorway. Where was the nearest exit? If I could just get
outside, I was probably free.

Unfortunately, the locker rooms were close to the casino,
an area specifically designed to keep guests away from the
outside world. I would have to either make my way all the
way around to the other side, near the restaurant, or I
would have to take an elevator to a different floor, then go
out through the lobby.

Since I was already heading down the hall towards the
casino, I figured it would look more suspicious on camera if
I suddenly bolted in the other direction, so I decided the
restaurant exit was the way to go.

The casino floor was fairly busy. Perhaps I could blend
in and disguise myself enough to buy more time. I saw a
gentleman in a cowboy hat playing the slots and I had an
idea. I walked up to him and placed my arm on his back.

"Hey there, cowboy, I like your hat," I purred.

He seemed slightly alarmed at the water stains on my shirt, but his eyes caught on my chest.

"Do you mind if I borrow it?" I asked, drawing my arm around to his chest, removing it from his head, and placing it on my own.

I smiled at him and before he realized what was happening, I strolled off, the hat hiding my hair and features from above. I strolled casually but purposefully towards the restaurant opening, my head down slightly to avoid the cameras. No one seemed to notice I was barefoot and damp. I kept going, in between the rows of slots, and past the tables and roulette wheels. The casino seemed endless. Almost there. Almost there. I was nearly at the restaurant now.

"Aren't YOU a slippery one!" From seemingly out of nowhere, a man was directly behind me, gripping my arms, pinning them behind me with one strong arm.

He pulled me backward a few feet into the hallway with Pete's office, where the folks milling about the casino floor couldn't see us.

Still gripping me tight, he knocked my hat off and let it fall. He leaned in towards my ear. "I am going to have some fun with you."

It was Bleid. His words held so much evil and malice, I couldn't help but feel the fear creep through me. I turned my face toward his, and before he could react, I bit his nose as hard as I could.

twelve

. . .

HE CRIED out and loosened his grip slightly, giving me just enough leeway to slip out from his grasp. I tried to run, but he caught my leg and pulled and I fell. My left side slammed into some kind of cart or table, and my chin struck the ground so hard that I bit my tongue. A fierce pain reverberated from my side, and I could taste the blood pooling in my mouth. I kept fighting him off, but he turned me around and straddled me, pinning me to the ground. I tried to reach my bag to get to my knife.

He backhanded me so hard I nearly blacked out, and then he began choking me. I closed my eyes and fought for my life, thrashing about, trying to get him off me, but he was so strong, and I was in so much pain. And then suddenly, he wasn't there anymore. He had let go completely.

I opened my eyes in time to see his eyes roll back in his head, and he slumped to the side. His nose was bloody from my bite, and a bit of blood trickled from his nostrils and his mouth. Above him crouched Ram, anger and strength pouring off of him.

Ram had just killed my attacker, but he still refused to

look at me. No matter what his deal was, he would not be on the cartel's nice list after killing one of them.

I sprang up, gathering my wits. I was dizzy, and my body screamed out in pain, but adrenaline kept me moving. We had to get out of here NOW, but hiding the body would be a good idea with so many humans around. I tried a nearby door and discovered a storage closet, and dragged his body into it. The pain was streaming through my side now, making it hard to breathe. Saying nothing, Ram finished shoving Bleid's body into the closet and closed the door behind him, then quickly wiped the doorknob clean of our fingerprints.

"We have to go," I mumbled through an increasingly swollen mouth.

I grabbed his arm with my right hand and pulled him along after me. He kept my pace but still acted as if I was invisible.

Has he been cursed somehow? What the actual fuck?

Twenty more steps, and we made it out the door.

"Hey!" Hydd burst out the door after us as we stood on the sidewalk.

I bolted down the street toward the parking garage, still pulling Ram along behind me. We ran for the elevator, the door closing just as Hydd rounded the corner and spotted us. I punched the button for level 3 and the door close button as fast as I could, and prayed Hydd wasn't a very fast step-taker.

Once the doors closed, I dug into my bag. My first instinct was to get my knife, but I realized pretty quickly that I also needed my car keys, and my left side was in too much pain to be useful for either. I decided my keys could do double duty. I put them in my right hand in a way that made me ready to unlock the car door or do some damage by punching Hydd's face with a key point—whichever came first.

After what felt like an eternity, the elevator doors opened. I peered around cautiously, and when I didn't see Hydd, I ran towards the car, once again, literally pulling Ram behind me.

"What is your fucking problem!?"

I mumbled, but it came out all garbled. My tongue and face were swelling up at a rapid pace. One eye was nearly swollen shut. I just hoped I could keep my vision long enough to drive us out of here.

Miraculously, we made it to the car just as Hydd arrived, panting from the top of the stairs. I scrambled to open the door, reached over, and opened Ram's side. He went around and got in, all the while not looking at me, acting as if he was in his own little world and I didn't just mumble for him to get the hell in the car.

I locked both the doors and fired my dream car up just as Hydd grabbed the handle and tried to open the door. I popped it into reverse and backed out as quickly as I could, forcing Hydd to lose a grip on the handle. I peeled away, going as fast as I dared down the ramp to the exit before anyone else could stop me.

As I approached the exit, the gate attendant was on the phone, staring at me. I suspected he was being given direct orders not to open the gate for us. I took my hand and placed it gently on the dashboard, petting my baby.

"So soowweee," I mumbled, words getting even more difficult, as I punched the gas and blasted through the gate, denting the hood and cracking the windshield on my way out.

I drove as fast as I could, taking a winding path to make sure no one was following us before I turned toward Henderson. Ram just sat there, continuing to look out the window, perched as far away from me as he could be. Things were pretty fucked up, but I was alive, damn it. *I made it out.* I let out a laugh, but it hurt badly. I suspected I may have broken a rib or two in the fracas.

————

We pulled up to the house and into the one-car garage. I think Revati was crying again, but I was in so much pain it was easy to ignore her. I stumbled my way to the door. When I was almost there, it opened, and Angel came out. The look on his face was haunting. It was devastation and pain entwined. He ran to me and held me. Now that I was out of immediate danger, the fear and the anxiety over Devil's fate and what it was doing to Angel wracked through me.

"They have him," He whispered. I nodded.

"I'm so sowwy, Angel. I'm so sowwy," I mumbled through my swollen mouth.

I couldn't stop crying. Angel got still. He must've noticed Ram. I tried to explain.

"This is Wam. He kiwwed Bleid, but…" my voice broke on the last word.

I thought about how to explain the situation: He was my ex, he was ignoring me, and he was in the cartel now. Each ending seemed more painful than the one before.

"Shhh… Sugar, let's get you cleaned up," Angel must've given some kind of sign to Ram because he followed us into the house.

Angel gently set me down on the sofa and fetched a soft wet cloth. He tenderly wiped the blood off my swollen face, got me some ibuprofen and a glass of water, and gave me an ice pack to hold on to the worst parts. I thought about Devil. The last thing I said to him was that I never wanted to see him again. A fresh round of tears started.

"Do you know where they took him, Sugar?"

"Echidna said they were taking him from dinner, but I…

wasn't there," I told him, trying my best to keep the words pronounceable. The swelling of my tongue was finally starting to go down a bit, though it was still very sore.

Explaining my personal issues with him to Angel was going to have to wait until after we found him. As upset as I was with him, he didn't deserve to die at the hands of these monsters.

"If he knows their secrets, they'll be keeping him alive. They won't want him going Upstairs, where he can report to the High Order."

Ram spoke to Angel, careful to look only at him.

"You were at dinner," Angel stated.

It was more of an observation than a question. Ram nodded.

"I was. They began by questioning you—him—about his love life. Then they mentioned his wedding on YouTube. Then he... yes, that's when he knew something was wrong, and he scribbled a message on a napkin and snuck it to me. You're his twin?"

Ram seemed to put the pieces together as he spoke.

"Something like that," Angel nodded.

"What did it say?" I asked, but Ram didn't respond.

He only looked at the clock on the wall instead. Angel looked at the two of us, then repeated my question.

"And the napkin said…"

"Owl. Crow. Nest."

In the High Order, there was a secret code between agents. They were all given bird names, and if you were told to nest, it meant you should abandon the mission and go to a safe house. Even though I wasn't officially an agent, I was given this information to help me safely escape should something go wrong.

Devil must have counted on Ram's past knowledge as an agent and hoped he would understand and help us despite his current involvement with the cartel. I thought about the dinner conversation, and our wedding, and how it could have possibly given us away. Then it hit me.

"Oh my God, I think I know how they know. Stupid, stupid!"

I jerked up to a sitting motion, closed my eyes, and breathed through the fresh round of pain. I grabbed the remote to the smart TV and turned it on. After some maneuvering, I found our wedding on the chapel's YouTube channel, an easy enough search.

No wonder they found it.

I wanted to skip through the vows. It was painful to watch that naive girl with fake lashes making promises about trust and love, but the video wouldn't load fast enough for the fast-forward button to work.

"We shouldn't have gone back this afternoon! You should have listened to me! So much pain we could have avoided!" Revati said.

Wow, thanks for chiming in. Helpful.

My swollen face didn't inhibit my internal sense of sarcasm.

Finally, the wedding was over. We danced down the aisle, and I stopped to blow a kiss at Agent Webber, his face entirely visible on the camera. I hit pause, his slightly smirking mug staying on the screen.

Ram stared at the screen and looked very surprised. It wasn't every day one saw Agent Webber looking pleasant. Surely, someone from the cartel recognized The Executioner.

I hung my head in shame. I had wanted him to be there. I had felt so much safer knowing he was staying in the room. That bit of foolishness had compromised the entire mission. I hadn't ever considered that the chapel might post a video of our wedding. Angel came over and held me.

"I told you not to flirt with him! Why did you ask him, anyway?" Revati was pushing all my buttons.

Stop, please. Gods, I'm sorry already! You were right, all-knowing Master!

"It's not your fault, Sugar. We all should have known better, including Agent Webber. I signed a disclosure promising they would not post it, but I suppose they did anyway, the bastards."

"But now Devil is captured, and who knows what they are doing to him," I was trying hard not to cry.

Angel took a deep breath. "Hurting him, Sugar. They are hurting him," and he squeezed his eyes shut.

I placed my hand on his cheek.

"You can feel it?" He nodded, then spoke.

"We need to call Agent Webber. He needs to know what happened. Maybe he can find where they have taken him."

Ram stirred. "I might know where they took him. Tell him to look below the Steakhouse. Take the stairs from the kitchen."

He spoke only to Angel, and still wouldn't look at me. Then he walked out the door. Revati and I both cried some more.

"Revati is sorry too, Angel. she says if she could help, she would." He gave a whisper of a smile for Revati.

"And if I could help with Ram, I would, Revati. He is your ex-husband, no?"

We both cried again as I nodded. What blubbering fools we were.

"If he comes back, I will try to learn more for you. There is a deep conflict there, but I'm afraid I was too preoccupied to get a clean reading on him. You said he killed your attacker, yes?" I nodded.

"But he won't look at me, or talk to me. It's like I'm… dead to him," I choked out the words.

Angel hugged me again. "But you're not dead, and I am so glad for it. We will fix this, Sugar. But first…"

Angel handed me his phone, and I felt ashamed. My

issues with Ram paled compared to what was happening to Devil. I dialed Agent Webber's number, the one he had me memorize. As the phone rang, I switched it to speaker phone.

"Yeah," he barked into the phone, picking up on the first ring. "Webber?" I said, trying to make my voice sound stronger than it was.

"What's happened?"

"They have him. They know."

There was a moment of silence.

"Are you safe?"

"I got out."

"Echidna?"

A pang went through my chest.

"Dead."

"We'll sweep the hotel, round them up, see if we can find him."

"Look below the Steakhouse, stairs through the kitchen."

"We'll start there. You at their place in Henderson with the nice one?"

With that one sentence, I realized that despite his foolish mistake in attending our wedding, Agent Webber was far smarter than anyone had given him credit for. He knew about both Devil and Angel, knew exactly where they lived, and even knew about their very different personalities. I nodded with my eyes closed, but then realized I needed to use words.

"Yeah," I managed.

"I'll be there then. Wait for me."

"Ok. Wait—" I stopped him before he hung up. "Bleid's body is in the hallway near the entrance. It's in a closet."

"We'll take care of it."

I hung up and set the phone on the coffee table. Well, it

kind of fell out of my hand. I was still very weak, and my side was killing me.

"Sugar, when did you last eat?" Angel asked.

"Not since yesterday," I admitted.

"Finally, a problem we can solve," He said. Then he gave me a very sweet smile and went to the kitchen to find me something to eat.

———

I must've fallen asleep while waiting for Angel. I woke with a start, remembering fragments of a nightmare. There was blood and violence, and golden eyes fading to black. I couldn't be sure if they were nightmares or just memories of this day. I looked at the clock.

11:38 pm. Yep, still the same day.

I pulled the blanket off Angel must've placed on me. There was a smoothie along with my glass of water from earlier. What a sweetheart he was. He didn't deserve to suffer like this. I sat up, wincing at the pain in the movement, and drank some of the smoothie, swallowing very delicately, and washed it down with the water. I decided to find the bathroom, then Angel.

I tried not to examine myself too harshly in the bathroom mirror. My face was not quite as swollen as it had felt earlier, but it was still bruised, and very tender. I tried to lift my shirt to see my side, but the motion hurt too much, so I gave up for now.

"Angel?" I looked around for him.

The place wasn't that big, so it didn't take me long to find him. He was standing next to the front window, peering out into the darkness. He turned to look at me as I came in. He had that same pained look as when I first got here. I snuggled up next to him, and we stood in silence for several minutes.

"He is coming," he whispered.

He didn't sound particularly relieved. I hugged him tight. A car pulled up and parked in the driveway. Agent Webber jumped out of the driver's seat. It was difficult to see details in the streetlight. He opened the door to the backseat and pulled out a bundle wrapped in a blanket.

Devil.

Angel went to the door and opened it. In the porch light, Agent Webber hardly resembled the man we had just seen in the wedding video. He was streaked with what appeared to be ashes and blood.

Definitely a God of War.

Revati agreed. I backed out of the doorway to allow him the ample room needed to come inside, and I hoped none of the neighbors around here had cameras.

He came through the door, grim-faced. A bloody arm escaped the blanket bundle Agent Webber carried and hung limp, the hand mangled and missing several fingers. Agent Webber walked straight past us to the living room. Angel pulled the coffee table out of the way, and he laid Devil down as gently as he could in the very spot I had just vacated, then backed away. Angel kneeled beside him and peeled the blanket off, speaking softly in French. I let out a gasp when I saw him. He was badly beaten. It appeared every limb had been broken and cut.

"He needs Idun's!" I cried, kneeling next to Angel.

"No," Devil spoke, his voice barely a whisper. With how he looked, I couldn't believe he was alive, let alone conscious enough to talk.

Angel leaned in close, and the two whispered in French, or perhaps in some other language known only to them. Angel sat up and looked at me with a look that could only be described as pity.

"Idun's cannot cure him, Sugar. We are finished."

He rose and went into the other room, leaving me with

Devil. One of his eyes was swollen shut entirely, but he got the other open.

"Sugar," he said, but it seemed to take a significant amount of effort.

"I'm sorry," I cried. I was sorry about this whole mess.

"The brrrown book. Our room. Shhhhhadowlands," he forced out, coughing out a bit of blood. Had they broken all his internal organs too?

"Shhh, it's ok," I said, trying to find a place to place my hand to comfort him without causing additional pain.

I settled on a few fingers on his forehead. He closed his eye again and seemed to concentrate on his ragged breaths. I touched Devil's forehead again, and he smiled a bit and said something in French.

"He's refused Idun's, then?" Agent Webber's gravelly voice from behind startled me.

"He's past that, sir," Angel said, coming into the room, holding a silver metal case.

Agent Webber's face went even grimmer, as if he knew exactly what the case contained. I wondered if I was the only one who didn't understand what it signified.

I got up and stood next to Angel, and he wrapped his arm around me.

"She gets everything, of course," he said, speaking to Agent Webber, who nodded solemnly.

"No no no… wait, no..." a cold realization settled in.

This was bad, very bad. Angel kissed my forehead, then opened the case to reveal two guns, each with a silencer on the end.

"Will you do us the high honor, sir?" Angel asked Agent Webber.

He gave a curt nod of agreement. Angel handed him the case with the guns. As Agent Webber assembled and inspected them, Angel turned to me and hugged me tightly as I bawled.

Our marriage may have been contrived, and I only knew them for a little over a week, but I found this gut-wrenchingly painful, even though I knew they were going to a higher place. Literally.

"Goodbye to you both. If you make it Upstairs, please come find us. We dwell in the place known as the Dark Garden," Angel whispered into my ear to avoid being over-heard by Agent Webber.

I went over and kissed Devil on the forehead. His breaths were even raspier.

"Sssshuugg.." he couldn't even finish his word, and I didn't make him try.

Angel sat down on the sofa next to Devil, lifting him upright so they sat next to each other, heads leaning against each other. Agent Webber approached, a gun in each hand. I quickly turned around and headed into the kitchen, numb. I went straight over to the kitchen sink, waiting for nausea to overtake me. A few seconds went by. I heard the guns go off at the exact same time. Agent Webber was a very efficient killing machine. No surprise there. I closed my eyes in a moment of prayer for them.

"You didn't throw up this time. Good girl!" I supposed Revati was attempting to cheer me up.

She seemed to take death much more in stride than I did. I tried to chuckle for her sake, but it just came out another sob, and my side was still shooting pains.

I heard footsteps enter the kitchen, and I turned around just in time to see Agent Webber raise the guns he still held in his hands. He was looking back and forth between me and the corner with the small breakfast table and two chairs. Ram sat in one of them. I hadn't noticed him when I had come in.

One gun was trained on him. The other one was pointed directly at me.

thirteen

· · ·

"YOU SON OF A BITCH," Agent Webber snarled.

He looked angrier and scarier than I had ever seen him, which was saying a lot.

"I have not violated the injunction, sir," Ram slowly raised his hands.

"But yet here you are."

"I have NOT violated the injunction, sir," Ram said again, his voice rising.

"What are you doing?" I let out, my voice feeling tiny.

"How long has he been here?" Agent Webber asked me, but he kept his glare toward Ram.

"I didn't know he was in the kitchen," I said.

"But you knew he was here? In the house?"

"Yes, but—" Agent Webber adjusted his aim and took the safety off his guns.

"Wait!" I cried. "He was with the cartel, but he helped us. He killed Bleid," I explained.

"With the cartel?" He glared at Ram some more. "Some vigilante shit?"

"Someone had to stop them. I thought the High Order wasn't doing anything. Clearly, I was mistaken. But I assure you, sir, I have NOT violated the injunction. Please, she doesn't KNOW. No one told her, she doesn't know! I have not violated the injunction." Ram alternated between desperation and insistency.

I spoke up. "What the hell does that mean?! What injunction? What is going on? Why do you want to kill us? I got all your fucking DNA. I completed the mission. Is it because I killed Echidna? Was that some kind of protocol violation? I know Manasa was banned from Earth, but it wasn't her fault! They trapped her somehow."

Agent Webber turned his gaze from Ram back to me. He appeared surprised. Perhaps he hadn't known I was responsible for the death of Echidna, or that she and Manasa were the same person.

Oops.

"Shut up, Girl!" Revati yelled.

But I wasn't finished running my mouth.

"And YOU!" I stopped my line of questioning directed at Agent Webber, turned, and pointed an accusatory finger at Ram, wincing as the movement caused a jab of pain.

"Look at me, for fuck's sake! Just talk to me for one fucking second, especially if we're going to die, anyway! Why are you doing this to me? I thought you cared. I thought we… had something! Do you hate me this much?! Ram! What the FUCK is going on!?!"

My voice rose in volume and turned more desperate and angry as I spoke. Ram continued to stare at Agent Webber. I dug my fingernails into my palms as I stood at the sink, trying to control myself. Agent Webber kept the guns in place, looked at me, then back at Ram.

"How long has it been?" He asked. His voice seemed slightly softer than before.

Ram glanced at the clock on the stove, then closed his eyes.

"221 days, 23 hours… and 59 minutes."

Agent Webber looked troubled as he trained his gaze back and forth between the two of us, guns still at the ready. If I was going to die after all I had seen and done today, I decided not to be a coward about it.

I stood up taller, ignoring the pain, and stalked toward Agent Webber until the cold metal of the gun touched my forehead. I stared him straight in the eyes. His eyes seemed to widen in alarm.

"Just do it already. You've all ruined my life, anyway. Just fucking recycle me, get it over with." I said, pointedly at both of them.

A few very long seconds went by. I stared at Agent Webber's face, refusing to back down.

"DO IT!!! Fuck ALL OF YOU!!" I screamed.

Dong… Dong… Dong… Dong…

The grandfather clock in the living room chimed, cutting through the silence. He let out a breath, lowered the guns, and stormed out of the room.

Dong… Dong… Dong… Dong…

I wasn't sure what to do with myself besides try to steady my hands. They started shaking the minute the gun left my forehead. I stood there, trying to think.

Dong… Dong…

In the next room lay my dead husbands/partners, somewhere else in the house was the agent who had just killed them and just nearly killed me without any explanation, and in the kitchen with me was Ram, my ex-husband who had completely written me off and had almost just died by my side. For once, even Revati didn't know what to say. She had gone quiet. I suspected she was a little afraid of me after my little showdown.

Dong… Dong.

On the 12th and final chime of the clock, Ram slid out of his chair and then sunk to his knees, his head in his hands, his eyes closed, as he let out some kind of strangled cry. He looked as if he had just completed some herculean task. And then he opened his eyes and looked directly up into mine, and spoke.

"I'm—so sorry—" He seemed to be so choked up with emotion he couldn't speak.

"Those Who Judge—They forbid me. I could not speak to you, could not look at you—couldn't even ask others. 222 days. If I failed, we'd both be banished. The thought of you getting killed—and not knowing where you would end up —" He hunched over, crying.

"See? I told you! I told you he had a reason!" Revati yelled.

I briefly closed my eyes to buffer the intensity of the moment. He sounded so distraught.

"Why did they forbid you?" I asked, opening them again.

Getting fired plus this? It seemed particularly harsh. He seemed to be pulling himself together a little better now.

"It is illegal to give High Order Iduns to a human. Normally, the punishment is the execution of that human. I argued you were not human, not technically, citing my past holding request as the husband of the goddess inside you as proof. But since the divorce, I had no say."

He stopped for a moment to catch his breath. I was confused and still had lots of questions, especially regarding the "holding request", but I let him continue.

"No one knows what to do with the Lost. They compromised with this 222 day sentence. I don't know why that long. I don't regret the Idun's one bit, but I don't understand why no one told you. At least I knew, I understood! I could count down the days. The hours. The minutes. But you—you didn't know—"

His voice broke with emotion at the end of his sentence. He took a breath and continued.

"When I got in with the cartel, I never would have

imagined you would be there. I wanted to destroy them for what they did to you. For the woman who died in the fire. For anyone who has suffered at their hands. And to see you there too, and to not be able to talk to you, to ask you why —to ask ANYONE why—"

I thought about what he must have been going through. He had assumed I knew about the punishment, and that I was perhaps dutifully waiting for him, counting down the days, or at the very least, that I understood what had happened. But to discover that I hadn't known anything, and had married into the very cartel he was trying to destroy, at least in part for what they did to me? It must've been maddening.

And yet he still managed to save me, all while ignoring me. And then we STILL almost got killed at the last minute. Quite literally. I was overwhelmed and didn't know what to say.

"Tell him I love him! Tell him I am here!" Revati was bawling.

"I've been dreaming of what I would say when I was finally allowed to speak to you again. I thought I had it all planned out. But now, with what has happened today, all I can say is that I'm so sorry, for all of it. Every last bit. If I could take away all the hurt and pain you've suffered this weekend, I would. I would do anything for you, Chuli." He said the last part with quiet sincerity, then he added, "Sorry, I mean Naoma. I forget sometimes."

He tilted his head and looked up at me again, tears and dirt and blood all smeared together on his face. It was the most beautiful sight I had ever seen.

"Chuli's good," I replied, barely a whisper.

I didn't know why, but a name was a powerful thing, and hearing my old name on his lips helped bring me back to myself from whatever this hellish life was that I had been living. And for the first time since I had seen him again, he lifted the corner of his mouth in the ghost of a smile.

"Chuli it is, then."

I walked the few feet that separated us. He was still kneeling. He leaned his head against my stomach, and I wrapped my arms around his head and shoulders the best I could. His arms came up and wrapped around my legs, and for just a moment, there was a ray of light on this, the darkest of days. The moment lasted all of a few seconds before it was interrupted.

"You...you...liar! You sneaky thief! Tell him about me! TELL HIM RIGHT NOW!" Revati began an ear-piercing wail.

The pain was nearly crippling.

Shut up, shut up!

"I won't shut up! I WON'T! You're stealing him! THIEF! THIEF!!" She screamed.

I stepped back before I lost my mind completely, my hands over my ears, as if that could help, but the movement sent a fresh wave of pain.

You've got to GO, bitch!

In my desperation, I recalled Devil telling me about the book of the Shadowlands. I hobbled up to the bedroom and locked the door behind me. I poured over the bookshelf until I found a small brown leather book. I paged through it, looking for anything I might need. It was very cryptic. It contained very few words—a few verses in a language I didn't know, and a couple of sketches. This was no "Field Guide to the Shadowlands, Lost Edition."

Someone may have been knocking on the door, but it was impossible to hear properly with Revati screaming.

"Shut up! Shut up! I need to think! Go away!" I yelled.

I wasn't sure if I had said it out loud or in my head at this point. I was completely breaking down. I reached into my bag and retrieved the little bottle of iboga. 5 pills were remaining.

I grabbed three and put them on my tongue. I planned to send Revati there first, so I could concentrate enough to absorb something from the book, talk my way out of this house of death, then somehow go to a safe place—a hotel, maybe.

Once I had a better understanding, I would take the remaining two pills and hope it was enough to join her in the Shadowlands. I figured 3 was the right amount to take just now, since the first time, it had taken 1, and the second, 2 pills to send her there. That was how tolerance worked, right?

Wrong.

Instead of Revati's screams fading, they got louder, and more insistent, as the edges of my vision turned black.

fourteen

. . .

I FELT like someone had thrown me down, but there was something soft below me. I was lying on soft ground, with some kind of grass or weeds tickling me.

I sat up and dusted my arms off. I could see my body clearly, as if I had a light glowing from within. It was not quite as sparkly and shimmery as when I was dealing with the after-effects of Echidna's kiss, but it was similar. I looked around, but everything else appeared black.

"YOU!" a voice came from behind me.

The voice did not resonate and did not travel far, as if the darkness had simply swallowed up the sound waves.

I got to my feet and turned around. A woman was standing there, a finger pointed angrily at me. Like me, she was glowing, although her hue was a perfect vivid golden hue.

She was perfectly composed and absolutely gorgeous, with long black shiny hair peeking out from behind a golden headscarf. Her long dress was emerald green and embroidered with shimmering flowers and vines. Her large dark eyes were thickly lashed and currently glaring at me. Her perfect mouth appeared to be clenched in anger.

My mouth seemed to hang open of its own accord. For a moment, I was completely wrapped up in her beauty and felt awed by her presence.

"Where is the book!?" she cried, her anger turning to alarm.

I looked down at my hands as if I expected it to materialize. Then I realized two things at once: Where I was, and who the woman was. I looked at her again.

"Revati?"

"Who else, you, you, DUMMY! What have you done!?" and she charged at me, furious, shoving me hard.

I lost my balance and fell over. She continued to attack me. Fortunately, I didn't feel the pain from my previous injuries here, so I fended her off, ripping off her headscarf in the process. Eventually, I got us turned around and got her flipped underneath me as I pinned her arms back, putting her in a hold. Somehow she still looked graceful and composed, whereas I must've looked like a disheveled nut case.

"Are you finished?" I asked, out of breath.

She nodded begrudgingly, and I let go and sat next to her. I was so tired, all I wanted to do was sit back down and have a big cry and go to sleep. But if this was going to be my only chance at ridding myself of Revati, I was going to have to suck it up.

"Ok, so... I screwed up. I'm sorry. But if you wouldn't have been screaming and I could THINK for a minute..."

"Oh, that's rich. Nice apology, stupid girl! You're blaming me! You steal my husband, and now you ruin my only chance at freedom?"

Her ire was coming right back.

"Ok so, ok... I really am sorry. I want to be free too, you know! And look, I'm not trying to steal your husband!"

I put my hands up in a defensive position. "It's—more complicated than that."

I didn't know how to sort my feelings out on Ram, and now was not the time to try.

Can you still hear my thoughts?

I mentally asked, out of curiosity more than anything. Revati didn't stir or seem to hear me one bit.

Well, at least there's that!

"Ok so…" I began again.

For some reason, that was just the catchphrase of the moment for me.

"We're both here. Let me think for a moment. Maybe we can figure this out. Let me think back. Let's see… Shadow-lands, Shadowlands…"

I couldn't recall any mention of the Shadowlands in any of the books we published back at Burning Wind, but I had edited a book on sacred hallucinogenic plants. I knew that iboga was cultivated by the Fang people. Their religious practices had a name, but I forgot what they were called. They had no written texts. I remembered they had some kind of multi-night festivals, where they ate iboga bit by bit until they traveled into the land of the dead.

"The land of the dead! That must be the Shadowlands. Oh, I think I know what happened, and why I am here. I must've still had iboga in my system from Saturday night. Gods—was that really only last night?"

I sat back a moment in wonder. It felt like a lifetime ago.

Revati just looked at me with an impatient look on her face, waiting for me to come up with something useful, I supposed.

"Ok let's see… there are some kind of spirits somewhere. And there is a God…Mebeghe? Who rules over all. And something with… an egg? Or triplets?" I recalled some kind of trippy illustration and a brief paragraph.

"You are useless." She rolled her eyes.

"Who speaks his name?" a thickly accented voice seemed to circle us in the dark.

We both jumped up in alarm and looked around. A glow seemed to appear from nowhere, beginning as a tiny wisp of a cloud circling us, until it became brighter and larger in size, eventually materializing into some kind of green-hued half invisible human-like shape.

It hovered near us. There were two orbs for eyes, glowing brighter than the rest of it. I bowed my head. I wasn't sure what the correct protocol was, but I felt like some kind of recognition was in order. Revati just stood there, making no effort to acknowledge the..whatever this was.

"I'm Naoma, and this is Revati. We've come for help. Is Mebeghe… around?"

The glowing came closer to me. It appeared to be smelling my hands. "Hmmm. Nice okandzo. Old school, eh? These days a chicken will do, but I like your enthusiasm. Perhaps he will too."

Okandzo... okandzo… chicken? I thought again about everything I knew. Yes, a sacrifice! That was it! They usually sacrificed chickens. But the original sacrifice was… Oh. He somehow seemed to smell the death of Echidna on my hands. Revati looked at me, confused.

"Sacrifice," I mouthed to her.

Her eyes opened wide.

"Follow me," he said and hovered off down a path just barely visible in his glow.

We walked along for what seemed like a long time, but it was hard to say. In the blackness, there was no keeping track of time or distance. I felt as if the surrounding shadows were watching, but no one else approached.

Eventually, we came to some kind of stone archway. I could hear running water nearby. We walked across a soft lawn of some sort, the running water sound getting louder. Finally, we arrived at the bank of the river and climbed down.

There, standing at the edge of the water, looking into its depths, was Mebeghe. He turned and watched us as we approached. He was wearing a silver robe, made of some kind of gauze that sparkled slightly when he moved as if it was sprinkled with stardust. His dark skin glowed and shimmered. His long, thin, white dreadlocks did not age him, and his eyes were the most vivid and deep shade of violet-blue I had ever seen. They were like periwinkle's sophisticated cousin. He was beautiful.

The spirit thing approached him in some kind of hovering bow and spoke some words in a language I didn't understand. I bowed low. I tried to signal to Revati to do the same, but once again, she just stood there. I supposed royalty didn't bow to each other, but I didn't know.

When I stood up, he was staring at me, and I self-consciously looked down at myself. I was filthy and blood-stained, wearing the same clothing. I felt like I had come to an interview woefully unprepared.

"Greetings, your majesty," I said, awkwardly.

He sniffed the air about me a bit, then stepped closer to me.

"You smell of death and pain." His voice was deep and rich. "Who are you, child? Why are you here?"

"Um, well, we—that is, Revati and I—and I'm Naoma, by the way, respectfully request your help, your majesty, sir," I was still aiming for some sort of formality, but his intense staring and his sniffing and the whole situation had me bumbling over my words.

He leaned over me and sniffed me in the way a dog might when its owner came home after spending time in a kennel. He sniffed down my arms, lifting my hands for better access. He leaned in and sniffed directly over my scar and made a strange face. Then he sniffed my cheek, focused on where I had been backhanded, and he damn near stuck his nose in my mouth to smell where I had bit my tongue. It was disconcerting, but I stood very still.

"Stop sniffing her, you, you… wild heathen."

Leave it to Revati to go straight for the insult. I swear he let out some kind of growling noise as he looked up to glare at her, and I felt the hairs on my arms and the back of my neck rising in alarm. He backed up a step and rose to his full height, significantly taller than me. I hoped talking might ease the tension.

"We were told, sir, that you might be able to help us? You see, she is trapped in my head. Well, she isn't right now, obviously, but usually, on Earth, she's in me. She was Lost. But now she's found. But stuck."

I had no idea if he was understanding what I was saying. He at least turned his gaze back to me instead of looking ready to attack Revati.

"Who said I would help you?" He asked me.

"Um, well, my husbands may have mentioned it,"

"Husbands?" He stood back a bit and gave me a different kind of once-over, relying on sight more than smell this time.

"Yes, but they—that is, they—" I tried to keep my voice resolute, but their death, even if it was only from Earth, was still incredibly fresh. If it had been paint, it wouldn't even be close to dry.

Mebeghe reached his hand out and wiped the tear spilling from my eye with the pad of his thumb, then put it in his mouth and sucked.

Nope, not creepy at all.

This act startled me enough to help me keep it together, and I continued.

"They can't help us now. So we're hoping you can."

He stood silent for a moment, as if he was considering.

"You wish to barter for her passage?" he said, and he

referenced a spot on the shore behind him I hadn't noticed before.

There was a dock of some sort, and a small boat with oars.

"Uh... I think so?" I said, nervously, looking at Revati.

She shook her head. "No, no way! I'm not getting in that boat without a real clear description of where it's going."

She crossed her arms and stamped her foot. Mebeghe ignored her.

"Where does it go?" I asked him.

"Does it matter? You will be rid of her insolence," he said.

She looked at me, eyes wide. "Yes, it matters!" she yelled.

Honestly, I wished it wouldn't have mattered to me, but I would not and could not in good conscience just send her off into the dark like that without guaranteeing her safety.

"Unfortunately, it does matter," I said to him, sighing.

There appeared to be a twinkle of humor in his eyes, and he smiled.

"Tell me what you can trade me, and I'll tell you where it goes," he said.

What could I possibly have that he would want? I didn't know anything about him or his world. No one did. There was just that cryptic little book. *Aha! That's it!*

"Have you heard of Burning Wind Press?" I asked him.

"Apollo's Earth books?" He looked intrigued.

"You got it. Well, I'm the one that makes it happen." I proudly pointed to myself.

"You? You are Paul's Lost?" I nodded.

I didn't realize I had my own special nickname. Paul's Lost. How... pathetic. I hitched up my self-confidence and kept going.

"I can offer you a book deal on the Shadowlands. After

that, who knows? Maybe even try to get a show based on you."

He laughed, and it boomed out before the darkness swallowed it up again.

"The boat takes you to the Bay of Stones. Dock there and climb the stairs. The path will lead you Upstairs."

I looked at Revati. She still seemed hesitant.

"And what about you?" she asked me.

"I'm only mortal. I belong on Earth. Plus, I now have a book to help write."

"Wait a minute..." she said, narrowing her eyes, getting closer to me.

"You just want Ram all to yourself! That's what this is about! You and Devil, you worked this out when you sent me away yesterday! You can't have him! He's mine! I'm not going anywhere!" She stomped her foot in anger.

"You would risk your only chance at getting back Upstairs just to be with him?" I asked, outraged.

"Of course I would!"

"I could take her anyway. Force her."

Mebeghe strolled over to her, his green ghoul friend appearing out of nowhere. Together, they picked her up and started dragging her over to the boat, kicking and screaming.

"Wait! No!" I said.

Here was a perfectly good opportunity to get rid of her, and I just couldn't do it. What was wrong with me?

"Mind if I talk to her for a moment?" I asked him.

They let go of her and took a few steps back.

"Are you really serious here? You won't leave? What if I promise to tell him what happened?"

She sighed. "I can't risk it, girl. I LOVE him. I can't just leave him on Earth! He cut his hair, he grieved for me. Our marriage connection was *dissolved*. If I don't stay, how will he find me again? He needs to know I am here, to rekindle his love for me. I need to be in his life, even if it's through you. Please," she added, her voice cracking as tears welled in her eyes, "I can't let him forget me."

I tried to sort out her logic, but what did I really know about true love and magic and weddings and gods?

"We'll have to find another way. Is there one?" I directed the question to Mebeghe.

"There is a way to give her life on Earth, but it requires power. Objects. Things that I do not possess. I truly wish that I could help you," and he looked at me again.

He seemed very sincere. I looked at Revati again, and I rallied my strength to do the right thing.

"Ok, fine, you can stay with me. But if you do, you need to promise to give me some respect and to let me tell him when it feels right to me. I'm barely hanging on by a thread at the moment, and I need some time to think this through. No more yelling at me. We need to work together, not fight each other. Understand?"

"I agree." Revati looked determined and maybe a little grateful. We shook hands on it.

"I'll still help you though, Mebeghe."

I don't know why, but as potentially dangerous as this god was, I still sensed he was good and meant no harm, and I truly wanted to help him, creepy sniffing and all.

"Write down everything you can think of about you, and this place, and come find me on Earth. We're moving our office, but when we reopen, your book will be our first publication."

He smiled and stood by me again.

"Child, I do not care about nor want a book."

I was confused. "Then what were we trading?"

He smiled again. "Nothing. You have nothing I want. You have not seen her, or I would smell her on you."

I could hear a hint of sadness in his voice.

"But you would still help me?"

"Is it so hard to think I might want to help you out of the goodness of my heart?"

"I..." I thought about it for a moment.

He was weird with the sniffing thing, but not unpleasant.

"No, it wouldn't. Thank you very much for trying. I'm sorry to intrude on you. We'll be going just as soon as I figure out how."

"Let me give you a parting gift." He reached down and took a small, smooth stone from the river and placed it in my palm, then closed my hand around it, and spoke quietly.

"This will bring you to the Shadowlands. Hold it in your hand and visualize yourself here. Speak my name, and I will join you if you'd like some company. If you require silence, simply stay silent."

I stared at him as I felt the smooth rock in my hand. He leaned forward, speaking even more quietly.

"She cannot follow this way. You can stay for as little or as long as you like, whenever you'd like."

He was giving me the gift of privacy, which at the moment felt like the most precious gift of all.

I was overwhelmed with gratitude. This god owed me nothing, yet he was giving me everything.

"Thank you," I said and gave him a fierce hug.

He seemed surprised and disconcerted at my hug, which was pretty funny considering he'd nearly put his nose in my mouth a few minutes ago. He awkwardly patted my back.

"See you soon," he said, and everything went black.

fifteen

. . .

MY HEAD BEGAN to spin wildly. I hadn't felt this nauseous since I was a binge-drinking college freshman. I groaned. I felt cold and hot at the same time.

"Chuli, Gods, you're awake, you're alive," Ram said from somewhere above me.

His voice vibrated through me as I tried to get my bearings. I tried to open my eyes, but it just made me dizzier. With great effort, I turned from my back to my side. I risked opening my eyes again and saw the nightstand next to me.

So I was back in Vegas, then. Back in the bedroom. Back to the extremely fucked-up situation I had accidentally and immediately departed from, probably just leaving my body in a heap on the floor. But someone had picked me up and laid me on the bed at least.

"Sick," I managed to say.

I got off the bed and made it the few steps to the en suite bathroom, just in time to throw up every last bit of anything inside me. I laid my head down on the cool tile and groaned again. I don't know how long I spent on that bathroom floor, alternating between shivering wildly, throwing up again, and sweating profusely. Surely death was better than this.

Ram had tried to comfort me, but the slightest touch had me flinching in pain. He had wanted to give me medicine of some kind, but I refused. I had been partying so much, and relying on so many drugs to get me through these past weeks, I figured I was now paying the price for it. I wanted to do it cold turkey and be done once and for all with all of this garbage.

At long last, my nausea finally ebbed. I was too weak to do much of anything, but I finally propped myself up against the wall near the toilet. I looked at the bright sunlight streaming in the window, then looked down and saw that I was still in the same awful stained silk shirt and jeans. They were beyond ruined at this point. I looked at the shower longingly.

"Welcome back," Ram's soft voice came from the doorway behind me.

I looked up at him. He looked haggard, with dark circles under his eyes. He at least looked like he had a shower and changed into some clean clothes.

As if he could read my thoughts, he said, "Agent Webber made me take a break to shower and change last night. He insisted that when you came back, my stink would make you sick. Guess I didn't scrub hard enough," he joked, referencing the toilet, but I couldn't even manage a smile. "He watched over you while I cleaned up."

I remembered staring down the barrel of his gun, and I retched into the toilet again, then leaned back with the last of my strength.

"I don't think you have to fear him. He may be The Executioner, but he is fair, as far as I've seen. And I swear, he even looked remorseful. I didn't even know that was possible," he mused.

I wanted to be understanding, but I was too sick and

weak for further rumination on the subject. I just stared at the shower again. As if he understood, he walked over and turned it on, then helped me to my feet.

"Ok! All better now, girl? It's time to work together! So, what is the plan? How will you tell him?" Revati wasn't yelling at me anymore, but her bright and cheery voice reverberated inside my tender skull, sending pain and nausea shooting through me. I seemed to be the only one suffering the wicked aftereffects of iboga.

"Not yet... please not yet," I mumbled weakly to Revati.

"You stay here as long as you need to," Ram said soothingly, believing I needed more time hovering over the toilet before I showered.

"Ok, fine. Get yourself together, girl. I don't want you throwing up on him. But we'll make a plan when you're better?" She asked, causing me to wince again.

"Promise," I mumbled under my breath.

Please..no more talking..it hurts.

"I promise," Ram said sweetly.

Bless his heart, he still thought I was talking to him.

"As soon as you're packed, we'll go to the airport. The jet is ready whenever you are. I'll be down in the kitchen," he said as he left, closing the bathroom door behind him.

My shower gave me a little more strength. Once I was out, I wiped away the steam in the mirror and looked closely at my face. My bruising was very slight, not nearly as bad as I'd initially figured it would be. My tongue only had a little bump where I had bitten it, and it was hardly sore. After taking another deep breath, I discovered my ribs weren't broken after all. My side was still sore, but not shooting pain like before. I examined my side and saw only light mottled bruising. I wondered if maybe my mental vacation to the Shadowlands sped up my healing somehow.

I donned my most comfortable outfit: a pair of leggings

and a soft tank top. It took me a while, but I fought exhaustion enough to get my bags packed. I wasn't willing to go back into the living room at all, so I may have left some things behind, but I didn't care.

With my new clothing, I needed a second piece of luggage, so I took one from the closet. It still felt unreal that this all belonged to me in my new role as Introspection's widow, but I couldn't stay here—not with everything that had happened, and I was just too tired to make any further decisions at the moment.

Before we left, I opened the garage door and flicked the overhead light on to stare at my beautiful, damaged car one last time. It seemed like a powerful metaphor that I had wrecked the only part of my time here that had any ties to my former life and childhood. I silently apologized to the car, kissed my fingertips, and then touched it and said goodbye.

Ram helped get my bags outside, where a limo was waiting to take us to the airport. He told me that Agent Webber had taken care of the bodies in the living room and that the whole place was going to be deep cleaned and locked up until I decided what to do with it.

I let Ram guide me onto the private plane. Instead of sitting across from me as Agent Webber had on the way to Vegas, he sat next to me. He doted over me the entire plane ride. Somehow, he got me some tea and fancy organic snacks, the same exact kind I had devoured on the ride to meet Sundar and Radha in the city earlier this year. I wanted to ask about them. I wanted to ask about so many things, but I was still so sick and tired that I didn't have it in me, especially because I didn't want to set off Revati, who was still doing a decent job of staying fairly quiet.

I kept fading in and out of consciousness. Ram helped me back off the plane and into a different waiting limo, where I stretched out and fell asleep yet again. Perhaps it was because the nausea was finally fading and I had some food in me, but this time I slept deeply.

When I finally woke up, I was in a strange bed. It was a small, sparse bedroom, with a painted hardwood floor and some woven rag rugs. There was a pretty quilt over me, and a sweet little desk in the corner with an antique chair and a gas hurricane lamp. There was sunlight streaming in a window, but I wasn't near enough to look out. It was very quiet, and I could hear birds chirping somewhere out the window. I rose and looked out at a beautiful pine forest. The sight, sound, and smells of the forest did wonders for my spirit.

"There you are, girl! About time you woke up!" Revati said with a bare hint of admonishment.

So it wasn't a beautiful dream then if Revati was still here. I decided to ignore her for now and finish taking in my surroundings. I realized I hadn't ever asked where the plane was going. I had assumed it was taking me back to New York, but what did I know?

In the corner was a mirror. I was still wearing the same tank top and leggings as earlier, but judging from the way the sun was coming in, I guessed it was actually the next morning. There was a plaid flannel robe hanging on the back of the door, and I put it on. Wherever I was, it was much cooler than the desert.

I looked again at the mirror, and I couldn't help but smile at myself. With my shorter curly hair and my plaid robe, I resembled my mom quite a bit. She had worn a plaid robe in the morning ever since I could remember. Gods, I missed her so much, I could almost smell her.

I decided to find out what this magical place was. I walked out of the bedroom and discovered I was in a small vintage cabin, with a cute little wood stove, currently un-lit, a sitting area with a few floor cushions and a small loveseat, and a back wall with a countertop, dorm fridge, and apart-ment-sized stove.

I went out the screen door onto a small porch with two chairs. There was a path leading through the woods, but no sign of progress or technology or cars, and only the sounds of nature. I stepped down off the porch and felt the cool earth and prickly pine needles under my feet and took the deepest, most grounded breath I'd taken in a long time.

I thought I heard someone laugh a familiar laugh, and I looked towards the curve in the path. I couldn't believe my eyes. Ram came around the corner, a cup of tea in hand, smiling. And next to him was my mother. She saw me at the same time I spotted her, and her face split into a giant smile.

"My baby! You're awake! And look at your hair!"

"Kunchen!"

It was the first time I had seen my mother in her new role, and it suited her so well that I no longer thought I'd struggle to call her by her new name. This was a new, beaming version of the human formerly known as Mom. She had always had a riot of thick waves and a wide variety of artsy clothing, but now her head was shaved, and she wore a maroon robe. Instead of detracting from her beauty, it only emphasized her beaming smile and rosy cheeks. She hustled to me and wrapped me in a loving hug, fluffing my curls for a moment.

She was so soft and safe and I was so shocked to see her that I immediately started sobbing and couldn't stop. She helped me inside and sat next to me on the bed and didn't try to stop me at all, simply rocked me and held me and told me it would be ok.

After I had no more tears left, she told me this cabin was mine to use as long as I wanted or needed to stay. It was on the grounds of the Buddhist Meditation Center she now called home. She told me that whenever I was ready, she would give me a tour of the grounds, and I could meet her new friends, and we could even go to the nearby town, but that for now, everyone would respect my privacy and leave me be.

As we were sitting, she noticed the wedding ring still on my left finger and touched it. "You wanna talk about this?" She reached out and touched the bruises on my face, "Or this?"

I wasn't sure exactly how much I could tell her, but I needed to come up with some kind of explanation. I figured she was connecting the dots in her own way that required very little explaining on my end. I'd allow her to think I was escaping some kind of abusive relationship. It was easier than the truth.

"It's over now. He's gone."

"I'm glad. And I'm here if you ever want to talk about it, sweetie. You know I've had my fair share of toxic relationships over the years. But for now, how about we go out and get you a nice cup of tea?"

We were just coming back out of the bedroom when I saw the shadows of two figures coming up onto the porch. My reflexes kicked in and I dove down behind the kitchen counter, eyes on the knife block on the counter, ready to weaponise if need be. Kunchen looked slightly horrified.

"What did he do to you, baby?" She said as she squatted down next to me.

"That's a very good question!" said a familiar voice at the screen door.

I jumped up and flew around the corner, now safe in Paul's arms. I started crying all over again as he and Stewie surrounded me. His love and soothing power seeped into me.

I was overwhelmed with amazement. All of the precious people in my life were here. I turned around so I leaned against Paul, his arms wrapped around me from behind, and I looked at Ram, who was standing near the stove with a sad smile on his face.

"This bastard right here," Paul said, "managed to do the right thing. He called us from Vegas, told us about the arrangements he made for you, and insisted we get our asses up here pronto. But Goddess, we would have come without any prodding at all. You know that. I was making the plans from the minute the phone rang. We'll stay as long as you want us to."

He kissed the top of my head and backed up a few steps and looked at my mother.

"Kunchen! WOW! The name and the place suit you to a tee! So nice to see you again!" Paul and Stewie both greeted and hugged my mother.

After some tea, we sat around to chat. I listened to the soothing sounds of their voices, but I had nothing to say. I'm not sure what Ram told them, but I think they all knew I wasn't ready to talk because no one asked me any direct questions.

At some point, I decided to get up and get some air outside on the porch. Paul came out with me.

"I suspect it's not a coincidence that you came back from Vegas right around the same time the news is all aflutter about a foiled terrorist attack at a casino?"

I'd have to check the news, but that seemed to me like a terrific cover-up. I had been wondering how the High Order was going to spin what had happened.

"Amazingly enough," he continued, "No civilians were harmed, and only a single terrorist was killed. The rest are in Homeland Security's custody. There were rumors they had a hostage, but the news couldn't confirm."

"Huh," I said, not sure what else to say.

"Also, word on the street is that the whole black market on Upstairs drugs has collapsed and dried up. You wanna tell me about your time out there, or is this a 'what happens in Vegas stays in Vegas' moment?"

I decided to give him at least something, so I showed him my wedding ring.

"I got married at the Elvis chapel."

He leaned down to admire my rings. "Felicitations! Will I get to meet your lucky spouse?"

I shook my head. "I'm already a widow," I said, half-whispering.

"I'm so sorry, love," he whispered as he gave me another long hug.

I almost cried again, but an exhausted numbness was creeping back in. Paul guided me back inside and talked everyone into leaving me be so I could get some more rest. Ram was the last to leave. I stopped him before he got out the door, placing my hand on his arm.

"You... I…"

I couldn't get any words out to begin to express my gratitude that he had done this for me, so I hugged him instead.

"Shhh, it's ok. You don't have to say anything at all. You just take this time to heal. I have my own cabin here, too. We'll talk whenever you're ready."

"It better be soon, girl!" Revati piped up, no longer willing to stay silent.

I backed up and nodded, wiping even more tears away.

───

It took about a week of rest, gallons of spring water, and a steady diet of lentils and soup before I was at least partly on the road to recovery. I was still a little weak and needed lots of sleep, but I didn't look or feel quite as bedraggled.

One afternoon, I was sitting on the two steps leading onto my front porch, reading the small brown book about the Shadowlands. I was trying to determine what would happen if I used the small rock from Mebeghe. Would my body stay here, vulnerable? Or would my physical body vanish?

I longed to go there for some true alone time, but I didn't want to freak anybody out, and I wasn't ready to share my secrets about my Shadowlands journey with anyone else. I was turning the page when suddenly, a large shadow blocked the sun.

I snapped the book shut and went for the paring knife in my slipper boot.

"I hope you won't need to use that," Agent Webber's gravelly voice mused from where he stood on the path.

My heart pounded in fear. No, a paring knife wasn't going to do anything to a god as powerful as this one. He'd have shot me before I even made it a step off the porch. In fact, the last time I had seen him, his gun was pressed against my forehead, because I had walked right up to him, daring him to kill me.

I was scared for myself that I had been in that dark of a place where I would even pull a stunt like that, but I was willing to keep up that impression. I didn't want to give Agent Webber the chance to consider that I might be afraid, so I casually placed my arm back at my side.

"Come to kill me again?" I asked as nonchalantly as I could.

He opened his mouth to speak, but I cut him off.

"Yeah, I know. You're just the Executioner and all that. No hard feelings," I said, my voice dripping with sarcasm.

I looked at my feet and clasped my hands. I didn't want to look at his face. I didn't want to know if he ever felt remorse. A few seconds ticked by.

"What do you want?" I asked him, finally daring to look up at him.

He was in his usual military outfit, blood-free this time.

"I came to pay you. And to confirm details on the report."

He shuffled some papers in his hand.

"Congratulations on catching all those terrorists. I hear the president might hand out medals to the homeland security officers involved. Great."

I didn't feel great about anything that happened in Vegas. The cartel was gone, but it just made me feel numb.

He shrugged his shoulders as if it was all no big deal.

"I owe you an apology," he added.

I didn't know what to say, so I didn't say anything. He continued.

"I didn't know they didn't tell you about the injunction. I wasn't at the hearing. I assumed you were notified, since your life was on the line. And I didn't realize you two... I would have said—no, I *should* have said something. I'm sorry."

Once again, I had that feeling that I was seeing a secret soft side of Agent Webber that I suspected most people didn't know existed. He seemed like he meant it, and I was tired of all this jadedness. It made me sad to see myself all snarky and sarcastic like this, so I decided right then and there that it was pointless to hold a grudge against him, so long as he was truly innocent in this. But I needed to make sure.

"There's something else I need to know before I forgive you." I braced myself. "Did you know about the bet?"

"Bet?"

"Why Introspection chose me. Did he tell you?"

"No, he just said you already knew him, and it had to be you. Just like I told you."

I breathed a sigh of relief. Yes, I couldn't exactly trust the man who nearly killed me, but I could forgive him.

"What aren't you telling me here? What is the bet?"

I closed my eyes and took a deep breath. The betrayal

was difficult to talk about, but to wrap up both cases, I knew I had to tell him.

"Intro—the one I called Devil,"

He nodded at this, and I continued, but I looked away, out into the trees. It was somehow easier to get the words out that way.

"He gave the Veruni to Zach. He got it in Belgium from someone named Tom or Tobias. But anyway, he, uh,"

I tried to force my voice to stay nonchalant. I heard Agent Webber suck in a breath.

"He had a bet with Zach. That Zach would fail to catch me, even with the Veruni. And when he failed, Devil would marry me, and it would be his name I—"

But I couldn't quite finish the sentence. I swallowed the lump in my throat, still staring at the trees for a few more seconds before I changed the subject.

"So… that's that then. Every one of those fuckers was creepy as hell, but you got them all? You have all the evidence you need, right? You got the muffin?"

When he stayed silent, my gaze left the safety of the trees to look at him. He was looking at the ground near his feet, and he lifted his head in a nod to answer my question.

"Yes. They are all in custody. They will all be judged."

"Echidna was here entirely against her will. She won't be charged, right? Do you need me to go into the details about what happened with that, or…"

"I'm going to list her as incidental damage. No one will ask questions. She wasn't tagged, so she's not in custody."

Incidental damage sounded horrible & clinical, and I sat still for a moment, trying not to think about the feel of her body thrashing beneath my hands.

His tone changed, dropping to a softer level as he came and sat down next to me. "You freed her, Naoma. You saved her. I'm so sorry you were betrayed in the process. You deserve so much more than this."

He sounded so sincere that tears sprung to my eyes, but I stubbornly wiped them away.

"I have something for you," he said, reaching into one of his pants pockets. What he pulled out surprised me. It was the lucky bracelet my friend at Armagodden gave me; the one I placed on her chest when she died.

"They're ok. And," he continued, while gently placing the bracelet in my hand, "they're still together. You were right, they are in love. When two souls love deeply enough, they always find each other, even before their knowledge returns. They materialized in the same holding cell. When she remembered her last moments, she begged me to give this back to you. I told her you took out the whole cartel. She said to find her Upstairs if you ever make it there. Her true name is Achelois."

It was really nice to get some good news. I clutched the bracelet and took a deep breath. I was glad she was ok, but I doubted I'd ever see her again.

"Hey, thanks for helping me back there on the strip. I didn't think through what would happen if I kissed someone with blood strong enough to kill. I was really out of it."

He waved his hand like it was nothing.

"Clever. The hair helped too. Great job."

He pulled out a stack of papers and a clipboard, and we went over a few details of the case. Fortunately, he didn't need very many, mostly just my signature on reports. Once that was done, he switched topics.

"Your health appears to be improving. I see the iboga has left your system."

I looked at him sharply. "How did you know about that?"

"You had the bottle in your hand when you passed out."

Oh. That was a pretty easy way to find out.

"Did it work?" he asked.

"What do you mean?" I decided to play dumb.

"You know what I mean. Is she gone?"

I opened my mouth, but I didn't know what to say.

"Tell him! See? He already knows anyway! Maybe he will help us! TELL HI—"

Fine! Just stop yelling and I will!

"No. It would have worked—I mean, it *did* work. She had a passage back. But she wouldn't leave him." I hung my head.

I probably should have lied to him, but I was just so tired of all the hiding. Agent Webber leaned in closer.

"He know yet?" he spoke very quietly.

Agent Webber was a very observant man, and now I was certain he knew who was inside me and all about her relationship with Ram. He was the first one in the mine after our very brutal and violent divorce, after all. There was no hiding the matching gashes on our chests, the ones we still both wore as scars. I shook my head.

"Soon. I just…"

"Ms. Bhatt, you've been through more than most seasoned agents see in a whole life cycle here on Earth. Don't be scared of someone else's love story."

Anger flared up. I wanted to argue with him that's not what I'm doing, but what pissed me off the most was that he was right. I'd been avoiding Ram since that first morning here. It was cowardly. I let go of my necklace of rings I had been nervously fiddling with and pounded my fist against the step instead.

He held out an envelope with my check and stared at the rings in the sunlight. There were six of them strung on there now—the four rings from my marriage to Introspection, Ram's wedding ring, and the gift from Echidna. Quite the collection.

As I took the envelope and tucked it inside the book

cover, he leaned closer to examine them. He looked at me questioningly, as if asking permission to look closer. I nodded, and he picked the necklace up off my skin and looked at the ring from Echidna with an expression on his face I hadn't yet seen and didn't know how to decipher.

"Is this…"

"Revati says it's a piece of Nagama—"

I stopped because we both said the word Nagamani at the same time.

"It was a gift, she… is it illegal to have it? Do you have to confiscate it? I'm sorry, I don't know the rules."

I had plenty of time this past week to do some research and talk to Revati about the ring with a tiny sliver of gemstone Echidna gave me. Nagamani was the Hindu name for a serpent stone: a stone with special properties believed to revive anyone suffering from the venom of a snakebite. There were various forms of serpent stones in many cultures throughout the world, but the one that hung around my neck was, apparently, a piece of the most powerful and legendary one I'd ever heard of or read about.

In the Hindu epic *The Mahabharata*, one of the main protagonists is Arjuna. In the story, he was killed by his son. As he lay dead, one of his wives, a Naga princess named Ulupi, retrieved Nagamani and placed it on his chest. The magical stone brought him back to life and freed him from a curse to boot. I didn't even pretend to know how Echidna and Ulupi knew each other, but Revati was certain I now owned a piece of that exact same stone.

Agent Webber still stared at me, though his face got softer somehow, with a glimpse of something warm and maybe sad beneath the tough exterior. But then he turned away and adjusted something on his boot.

He turned to face me again, gently lifted my foot, and pulled off my fuzzy slip-on boot, the one with the knife in it. He lifted my pant leg. His hand was large, warm, and rough. He strapped a small knife and holster to my leg, then covered it with my pants and boot, setting the paring knife aside.

"Learn how to use it properly. It's a different throwing technique than darts. It has to spin. It takes more practice. Self-defense classes should help with that helpless feeling. I suggest you learn about guns too. It's much easier than stabbing or smothering. Less... feelings to process after-ward. Less pain."

For a moment, my soul felt completely bare. Somehow, this gruff, gravelly military god seemed to know more about what I was going through than anyone else in the world.

"Would you teach me?" I asked, surprising all three of us—Revati, Agent Webber, and myself.

He stood up and backed up a bit. "No."

Before I could react or say anything further, he stepped into the woods and seemed to disappear.

I looked at the substantial check. Clipped to it was the business card of the High Order's lawyer who could help me sort out all of my belongings in Vegas, including the house. There was another card from a specialty motor shop, with a note that they had repaired my car and were storing it until I retrieved it. I smiled at that.

Next, I removed the blade holstered to my leg. It was gorgeous and ancient looking and made of a material I'd never seen before. It was either stone or crystal. It had several small stones and what appeared to be a piece of amber embedded in the hilt. It was small, extending just a little bit past the tips of my fingers, but it practically hummed with power as I held it across my palm. It seemed so powerful and magical that I thought for sure it must have its own name, and I wondered what it could be.

I might've been a mess, but somehow I knew now that

things were going to improve. I would talk to Ram and let the chips fall where they may. Agent Webber was right. I had been through too much to let their love story sideline me further. With weapons and self-defense training, I would no longer feel so helpless and vulnerable. I didn't want to think too hard about how I would use those skills in the future. In the meantime, I had a peaceful place to stay and loved ones around me. Things were going to be ok.

———

triage: book 3

. . .

NAOMA BHATT IS FINALLY on a healthier path of healing from her past misadventures. But when Ram disappears under mysterious circumstances, she travels to India, determined to save him from the clutches of a deadly demon. Is she truly ready to face such a foe?

Visit sararuch.com for release information, a compendium of characters, and more!

about the author

Sara Ruch's tarot cards used to tell her she should stop living in a fantasy world. She didn't listen. Instead, she writes about the worlds she creates, sometimes fictional, sometimes not. She lives in the mountains of Pennsylvania with her loving and supportive family and friends, a few furry & feathered creatures, and all the flora and fauna a woman could ask for.

For more information including a compendium of characters, their origins, and how to pronounce their names, visit sararuch.com

acknowledgments

When I published book one of this series, I wasn't expecting so much love & support that the Universe could hardly hold it all! Thank you so very much to every single one of you that bought, read, shared, sold, and/or reviewed my book. Special thanks to those of you that made my first book signing so magical! Maybe that Veruni was a love potion after all, because I sure do love you all!

For this book, I'd especially like to thank Bob for his Elvis wedding experience, Amy for her insight into Vegas living, Erin for his expertise on Brooklyn neighborhoods, and Shane & Claire for their French fluidity. Thank you Jessica for the proofreading, Brooklyn know-how (including bringing me true Brooklyn bagels, YUMMMM!) and overall cheerleading. Kristin, thanks for helping me with the blurb, web stuff, and always letting me work out my own problems by texting you, haha! Amarynth & Kevin, you are my editorial dream team. And Ethan, thanks for always being my "Ohhh, what if THIS happens!?" spoiler soundboard (if anything happens to me, ask him what happens next! He knows!) Thank you all for continuing to follow along on Naoma's adventures!

Made in the USA
Middletown, DE
17 October 2023